Highwood

A Second-Chance Christian Holiday Romance

Montana Pet Rescue Romance
Book 2

Gayle M. Irwin

Also by GAYLE M. IRWIN

Montana Pet Rescue
Highwood Holiday

Pet Rescue Romance
Rescue Road
My Montana Love
In the Shadow of Mount Moran
Paws-itively Love
Pet Rescue Romance - Yellowstone Country Boxed Set
Finding Love at Compassion Ranch
Grams' Legacy
Rhiann's Rescue - Pet Rescue Romance Series Prequel
Paws-ing for Love: A Pet Rescue Christmas Story

Wyoming Pet Rescue Romance
Tails of the Heart

Standalone

Love Takes Flight

Watch for more at https://gaylemirwin.com/.

Lake Solitude Media
Casper, Wyoming

Hannah

I drove my Toyota 4-Runner down the half-mile paved lane toward the JBarN ranch house. My meeting today with John and Nadine Hanson regarding their fortieth anniversary celebration made me perspire a bit more than the previous five meetings. The event for which they had hired me was six days away. All systems were go – we just had the floral centerpieces, the hors d'oeuvres, and the drinks to review before I confirmed the final orders with the florist and the caterer. I had full confidence in the people I'd hired and normally, my confidence was secure. But this event with these people gave me greater anxiety.

Although my nerves increased during the final week of an event I've planned, much of that mingled with excitement. This time was different however, because I knew the Hanson's son would arrive in a few days. Although I had known he would attend the anniversary celebration when I accepted the job, the six weeks since saying 'yes' went by much faster than anticipated.

Six days. I had less than a week until I saw my ex-boyfriend. The last time I laid eyes on my clients' son was seven years ago.

Micah John Hanson. Middle name for his father. First name for the rugged area of Montana and the rough life ranchers often experience, from the days of the old west when his great-great-grandfather staked a homestead beneath the peaks of the Highwood Mountains.

Micah John Hanson, heir to the family ranch built up by the homesteader and the three generations that came after.

Micah John Hanson, well-known and successful bronc rider on the rodeo circuit. He knew horses and he knew how to ride them. But the rodeo was the object of my wrath because Micah chose that life over the one I thought we would share together on the family ranch. I was eighteen when Micah left to pursue the gold belt buckles. He loved horses and the limelight, and I loved him.

Micah John Hanson. Handsome. Gifted. Famous. Married with a son and later divorced. Still bronc riding and still sought after by women. Yes, I tracked him on the internet, but only occasionally. Well, maybe more than that, especially since his divorce. And now that his parents employed me to put together a special fortieth anniversary celebration for them, I wanted to know more about the man I would encounter at that party.

As I pulled into a parking spot to the side of the large, log ranch house, I prayed I would not see Micah until the night of the anniversary celebration. I'd be meeting with his parents one more time beforehand, and I silently asked God to postpone my former boyfriend's arrival to another day.

I called on God a lot for this project. I even almost turned it down, but Mrs. Hanson's appreciation of my work for another local couple's fiftieth anniversary earlier in the year and my aunt's animal rescue summer festival and fundraiser made me brush aside the fact I still harbored resentment toward her son. After all, it wasn't Nadine's fault, or her husband's fault, that Micah John Hanson was a cad.

I turned the engine off and took a deep breath. As I exhaled, I prayed aloud.

"Lord, thank you for the opportunity to help Nadine and John celebrate this special day. Help us to finalize what needs to be done and bless all those who are helping make this anniversary extra-special. I ask again – please don't let Micah arrive on our last meeting day Thursday. Let me know if I need to change it to Wednesday. To keep myself focused on the tasks at hand, it would be easier to run into him in a crowd at the party, a neutral location, than while I'm with his parents at the house."

I took a deep breath and then exhaled before I continued.

"Again, thank you, Lord, for giving me this job and your favor with Micah's parents. Thank you for your strength, grace, and love. Help me through the rest of this week, and may the party be extra-special for all who come, but especially for John and Nadine. Let me be your instrument in their happiness. Thank you, Lord. Amen."

I took another deep breath. Micah. As handsome at twenty-five as he was at eighteen, even more so. His maturity and time on the circuit, and likely here at the ranch, built his muscles and torso. Photos didn't lie – the man was a hunk. No wonder he dated, and later married, a model.

Before I traveled farther down that path, I shook my head.

Micah is next week's problem.

I exhaled.

Today, just another meeting with the happily-still-in-love couple.

I stepped out of the vehicle.

"Welcome back, Hannah!"

I pasted a smile on my face, turned and looked toward the home's wrap-around deck. Nadine smiled and waved.

"Coffee's on, and I have scones and huckleberry jam."

"Sounds delicious! I'll be right up."

I turned back to my vehicle and grabbed the multi-colored bag that held my electronic tablet and my purse. An image of who should have been my in-laws flashed through my brain.

Nadine, as sweet as the apple-cinnamon bread my Aunt Eileen makes, but still a rancher's wife who could ride horses and brand cattle as easily as any of the ranch hands she and her husband employed. John, a weathered, sunbaked fifty-eight-year-old who learned the workings of the land and livestock from his father and grandfather, the original John Hanson. Four generations of Hanson men, three named John and

Edward John Hanson, the original owner, built and grew the family holdings. One day Micah would take the reins. I wondered how long it would be before he accepted his legacy, left the rodeo circuit, and settled on the ranch for good?

I shook my head as I shut the car door. *None of my business nor concern. That horse left the barn seven years ago.*

I shut the doors on the 4-Runner and planted a smile on my face. Then I turned around and looked at Nadine, waiting for me on the porch. I walked the short distance to the wooden stairway that led to the deck and climbed up those steps and onto the porch. No leaves littered the flooring so either Nadine or John must have swept autumn's vegetation earlier in the day. She met me with a hug, and I returned the embrace.

TWO HOURS LATER, SITTING at the kitchen island of the Hanson's home, I closed my red-covered electronic tablet, gave my clients a smile, and said, "I think I have everything I need to finish up before Saturday. I'll check in with you once more, likely Wednesday or Thursday, for any last-minute changes you might have regarding decorations, music, etc."

John looked at his wife.

"I don't foresee anything, do you, honey?"

Nadine shook her head.

"No, but I'm grateful you'll do that, Hannah. You have the number of guests, right? And the number of tables we need?"

I nodded and patted the tablet.

"All right here. I'm glad you told me about your cousins in Malta. I'll make sure there's another table added with the appropriate number of chairs."

"Goodness, me! I couldn't believe Sheila dropped that on us last minute!"

John patted his wife's hand and said, "We'd have found space somehow, Nadine. There's always room for a few more guests."

I nodded and smiled.

"I build in a few extra tables just for situations like this. Believe me, they happen all the time."

I rose from the barstool and the Hansons followed suit. I extended my hand.

"I'll be in touch."

Mrs. Hanson clasped both of her hands around mine.

"Thank you so very much, Hannah. You've been a God-send."

I smiled and responded, "Well, I don't know about that...."

"We do," her husband interjected. "We know it can't be easy working with us after Micah ... well, after all that happened...."

Although it was difficult, I retained my smile and said, "Oh, that was so long ago. We've moved on."

Certainly Micah has. Marrying the model. Having a child.

I disengaged the heartbreaking cobwebs.

"I know we've purposefully not talked about it, but you know he's divorced now, don't you?" Mrs. Hanson asked.

I nodded and responded, "I'm sure the whole country knows. It's been a few years, though, hasn't it?"

Micah's father responded, "Nearly three. He's finally made peace with Ashley leaving, and he's gotten back out on the rodeo circuit. But he's promised to come back to the ranch to stay next year."

"Bobby will start kindergarten next fall, so Micah's going to finally settle down as he promised to do after the boy was born," Nadine stated.

I took a few steps away, an attempt to end the conversation.

"Well, I certainly wish him and his son the best. I'm sure his wife's leaving was hard on both Micah and the boy."

"Bobby hardly remembers his mother. She hasn't come around or written a note, anything, in the past few years," John said.

I shook my head. I did feel sorry for them, Micah's son, especially. Like a smoldering fire in a hearth, the conversation had stoked up too many painful memories, so I inched a bit closer to the kitchen doorway.

"Well, I need to get back to town and check in with the caterer and florist. If anything else comes up before our meeting later this week, please reach out. I'll do the same."

"Thanks again, Hannah," Mrs. Hanson said. "You're doing a wonderful job."

"I'm happy to be of service for this special occasion. What day would be better for you for our final meeting? Wednesday or Thursday?"

Before either could answer, I cocked my head. Did I hear a vehicle drive up near the house?

"Wednesday might work best," John said. "I have a water district meeting on Thursday."

A car door slammed. The three of us looked at one another.

"Who in the world...?"

Nadine didn't get to finish her sentence before running feet on the deck overtook her words. The kitchen door burst open and a tornado whirled through in the form of a young boy.

"Grandma!"

"Bobby!"

Nadine's happy voice also contained surprise as she swept the child into her arms. John, a grin on his face, embraced them both. My throat tightened. Heavier boots pounded on the deck and I closed my eyes.

Lord, no!

My palms grew sweaty and my heart lurched. I opened my eyes and looked for another exit.

"Hey, mom – whose 4-Runner is that out...?"

The familiar, deep, male voice trailed off.

I bit my lip and turned from gazing out the living room window. My eyes swept over the sweet scene of an elderly couple hugging their grandson and landed on the face of the six-foot-two, burly frame standing in the doorway.

Our eyes met. Dark chocolate met hazelnut. My mouth formed an "O" as I stood less than a foot away from Micah John Hanson, a man I hadn't seen in seven years, a man I never stopped loving.

Micah

C*an't be.*

I continued staring into her eyes. Those magnificent, magical eyes that reminded me of caramel candies. Her black hair was cut shorter, but I would know her anywhere.

The woman I left seven years ago.

The woman I'd never forgotten.

"Hannah."

I whispered her name. *Why is she here?* Last I knew she lived in Seattle. *Not that I followed her online,* I found myself lying to myself once again.

In spite of numerous flings, including with my son's mother, Hannah always had my heart. Now she stood here, in my parents' kitchen, the same kitchen I'll be in much more often after the end of the year.

"Hannah," I said again, this time louder.

I took a few steps toward her.

"It's, uh, it's good to see you again. What brings you back to Highwood Hills?"

Before she or my parents could answer, my younger sister's carefree voice came from behind me.

"Hi, ho, everyone! We're back!"

Jill stopped, mouth agape. I elbowed her in the ribs.

"Our parents have company."

"I see that," she responded in a lower tone.

Jill composed herself and said in a steady yet excited tone, "Hannah! My goodness! It's been a long time."

"Yes, it has."

My former girlfriend stepped toward Gillian and me and held out her hand. My sister, whom everyone calls 'Jill,' extended her hand as well, and then she pulled Hannah into a hug. At first, Hannah hung back, as if in distrust. I couldn't blame her.

Still, why was she here in my parents' house?

Then I noticed Hannah and Jill embraced each other like long-lost sisters. In a way, they were – or should have been – and that 'should have' was all my fault.

After embracing my sister, Hannah fixed her eyes back on me, hand extended in greeting. She cleared her throat.

"Nice to see you, Micah. It's been a while."

"Yeah, yeah it has."

As I enfolded my hand in hers, I felt her arm tremble. I looked at her face, trying to read her thoughts. Although a smile greeted me, it, too, wavered and her light brown eyes showed no light. My mind and heart flashed back to our late teenage years when Hannah's eyes danced and sparkled.

I realized this meeting was unexpected to her as well as to me.

"You're back early."

My mother's statement echoed in my ears.

"We weren't expecting you until tomorrow," she said.

Ah. That was the answer.

"Grandad, who's that lady?"

Bobby's nearly-five-year-old voice wasn't muffled. Like his great-grandfather, my grandad, my son spoke his mind.

"She's helping me and your grandma plan our party for Saturday night."

These first words out of my dad's mouth since Bobby and I walked into the house caused me to look at him. Hannah dropped her hand from mine. I looked at her again. She nodded.

"I'm the planner they hired for the upcoming anniversary celebration," she said.

"How cool!"

My sister was also a mind-speaker. I used to be. Until it got me into trouble as a younger man. Now, I listened to my parents' wise counsel and the counsel of my pastor. Except for Ashley leaving, my life had gone much better since I became a stronger Christian and listened, or took a deep breath, before I spoke or acted.

"I'm so excited you're an event planner, Hannah," Jill said. "Mom and Dad have helped me keep up-to-date with your career in Seattle, and when they told me you had moved back to Highwood Hills, I was hoping to run into you."

I gazed from my parents to my sister and back again. Seems I had missed that family memo.

"I just didn't think I'd run into you here, at our house," Jill finished her train of thought.

Train wreck might be a better way to put it.

But Hannah didn't seem dismayed or offended. She gave Jill a smile, one more sincere than she had given me a bit ago.

"Well, they've entrusted me with their special celebration, and so I'd better get back to town – I have a lot of meetings ahead as we finalize the event."

My son walked up to my former girlfriend, stuck out his right hand and said, "Hi. I'm Bobby. What's your name?"

Hannah appeared taken aback for a second. Then she smiled and extended her hand, saying, "I'm Hannah, Hannah Donovan,. It's nice to meet you, Bobby."

"Nice to meet you, too," my little boy said in the polite manner his grandparents and I had taught him. "My full name is Robert Micah-John Hanson, but most folks call me 'Bobby.' You can, too."

"Thank you, Bobby. I'm honored to know you."

"Why?"

We all stared at the still-four-year-old.

"Why are you honored to meet me?" Bobby asked. "I haven't done anything nice for you. Not yet anyway."

Hannah squatted down to look Bobby in the eye.

"Well, a person doesn't have to have anything done for them to be honored to know another person. I would tell the president of the United States or the King of England it was an honor to meet them even though they hadn't done anything nice for me. You know about God, right?"

Bobby nodded his head.

"Well, God's word tells us to honor others before we honor ourselves. So it's an honor to meet you, Bobby Micah-John Hanson."

She smiled at him. Hannah's beautiful smile always lit up her face, giving her an angelic glow. I observed that same appearance as she looked at and smiled at my son.

Why did I have to think about that now?

"It's an honor to meet you, too, Miss Hannah. Or is it Mrs. Hannah?"

Oh, son! I wasn't sure I wanted to hear her answer.

I looked out the large living room picture window. Several horses grazed on the green-gray hillside. I tried to think about the beauty of the autumn day, with the changing leaves and colorful grasses and shrubs. I wanted to look at and think about anything other than what was transpiring in my parents' home.

Hannah replied, "Miss. Thank you for asking."

My head whipped around and I stared at her again.

Could it be? Is Hannah really single?

My heart thudded in my chest so loudly I barely heard her say goodbye. Now it was Jill's turn to elbow me in the ribs.

"Good to see you again, Hannah," I heard myself say.

But was it? Was it good? For either of us?

Hannah

I felt the tears pinch the corners of my eyes before they rippled down my face. I had kept my cool inside the house, but I couldn't stay composed after jumping into the 4-Runner's driver's seat and traveling back up the road toward the highway. Once clear of the Hanson's view, pools of water came to my eyes and traveled a pathway down my cheeks like Highwood Creek during spring snowmelt.

I had told Micah's parents seven years had been enough time to get over their son. I lied to them and to myself. Though I'd put on a brave face every time I'd met with Nadine or Nadine and John, the butterflies in my stomach took flight. Until about two weeks ago. I thought the nervousness and anxiety had lapsed. But then today, God had the last laugh by waltzing Micah through the doorway ... and back into my heart.

"Why, Lord?" I whispered. "Why now? Why today? Why couldn't he have stayed away at least one more day?"

Silence. I then remembered my paternal grandmother's advice after my parents' unexpected deaths in a private plane crash.

"Our 'whys' won't get answered this side of heaven, honey. We can wonder and plead, but until we see Him face-to-face, we can't know the answer to everything, especially 'why.' Just ask Him to help you get through each heartache, each tragedy, each tough situation. He will for He promises to never leave us or forsake us."

Although I cried for days and weeks, and a few times as years went by, I clung to my grandmother's guidance, so that even after Micah left me for the rodeo circuit, even when I learned of his marriage, I let myself cry but not question.

"God promises to make all evil against us work out for our good," Aunt Eileen had said back then. "Keep trusting Him. Perhaps He has someone else in mind for you, someone you'll meet in college or when you start your career."

But that hadn't happened. No one had impacted my heart like Micah. But then again, I'd stayed busy building my career and I had kept my heart protected.

I arrived in town less than ten minutes after leaving the Hanson house. I composed myself enough to stop at the florist. Chloe Baker, the owner and my best friend, bid on the project and impressed John and Nadine with her ideas for the table center pieces and autumn-themed displays. I've been excited for her to secure this large project. We're both small businesswomen and we help each other when we can.

I walked into the shop and found Chloe waiting on a customer with another one standing in line. I caught my friend's eye and we nodded our heads at one another in acknowledgement. I took a seat at the high-top table used to display cards for sale. I pulled out my phone and scrolled through messages and missed calls. One call came from my cousin, Emma, my assistant when I plan large events like this anniversary party. I also received a text from the caterer and another from the resort manager. I responded to their messages.

I'm at the florist's now and will be in touch with you soon. I just finished meeting with the Hansons and there are a couple of additions to the guest list. I'll reach out soon to meet with you.

I just love technology! That small businessperson in me relishes finding ways to do two or more things at once, like how writing one text, coping it, and replying to the next person with the same message. So handy!

I noticed a voicemail left from a number I didn't recognize. *Oh, those spammers!* Because of my business, I always listen to voicemail because I never know if what I think is a spam call could actually be a potential client.

I glanced toward the cash register counter. Chloe was still with her last customer, so I took the opportunity to listen to the recording. I sucked in my breath as I heard that familiar male voice.

"Hey, Hannah. It's Micah. Mom gave me your number and I just wanted to apologize for the surprise entry. We weren't due in until tomorrow, but Jill was antsy to get back home, so we drove through the night from the event in Nevada. Bobby also wanted to get back and see his grandparents. Anyway, I'm sorry we surprised you. Obviously, I ... we, me and Jill, were surprised too. I also wanted to thank you for taking on this anniversary party for my parents. As we've learned from my brother's death five years ago, you can't take life lightly – a person should celebrate and be grateful for each day with loved ones. So, I'm glad you've been helping them make this year a special one for them. Anyway, thanks again for being part of mom and dad's celebration. See you at the party ... if not sooner."

I stared at my phone. Caleb. I had been living in Seattle when the older Hanson son died from injuries received in an automobile accident. Aunt Eileen had informed me and suggested I attend the funeral. I didn't. I couldn't. I knew Micah would be there, and he was married. I just couldn't bring myself to see him with his model-for-a-wife. I wasn't a model, and I'd never be one. Ashley Marie Barrett-Hanson was, still is, stunning. She's graced the covers of plenty of magazines, including the swimsuit edition of *Sports Forever*. No wonder she'd caught Micah's eye ... and captured his heart.

I had sent flowers to Caleb's memorial service and a sympathy card to his parents, and I included Micah and Jill in my hand-written sentiments. I had received a thank-you note from Nadine several weeks later but had never heard from her again. A chance meeting at the local grocery store eight months ago reconnected us, sort of, but it was the Miller's fiftieth anniversary party that brought the request from Nadine and John to plan the celebration of their special celebration.

Now I had a voicemail. From him.

How should I respond? Do I respond at all?

"Hey."

Chloe's voice caused me to look up from my phone.

"Important message?"

"Yes. No. I don't know. Maybe?"

Nope, can't hide my confusion. Even Phoebe from 'Friends' could pick up on it.

Chloe sat down in the bistro-style chair across from me.

"Okay, spill," she said.

Chloe had been my best friend in high school. Even though I'd been back in Highwood Hills for less than a year, I couldn't hide anything from her. I couldn't even keep my office stalker experience a secret after I'd returned to Montana.

I looked at her for a quick moment then glanced around the shop. No one around. I took a deep breath and, before speaking, I exhaled. Then I told her the whole story.

Micah

I hope I said the right words.

I'd often wondered what I might say if I ever saw Hannah again. I replayed the potential scenario many times in my head. But after several years, and especially after meeting Ashley, I stopped thinking about it. Hannah lived in Seattle, and I had a new life. When Ashley told me she was pregnant, at first I wanted to bolt. But I knew my parents would be quite disappointed if I didn't own up to my responsibility. I was raised better than that.

When Ashley told me she wasn't sure she wanted the baby, how pregnancy would mess up her modelling career, my heart broke. I told her I'd take care of her and our child. I was just as responsible for the situation as she was. I told her ranching was not the only thing keeping my parents on the land in Montana, that we had oil on our land, so money wasn't a problem. The oil company paid us well, so she would never have to worry. If she wanted to model again after our baby was born, that was fine with me, but if she didn't, if she wanted to be a stay-at-home mom, that would be fine with me, too.

"I don't want you worrying about money," I had told her. "You don't have to work again if you don't want to. You'll be okay. We'll be okay. Our child will be okay."

She appeared relieved. She had a rough pregnancy, a lot of sickness, but when our son was born, we were both happy. Or at least I thought we were.

Two years of living first on the road and then at the ranch, even with her returning to modelling part-time, didn't fit with the life she wanted, she told me in year three. Bobby was just two-and-a-half. We had named our son, Robert, after Ashley's father, who had passed before our boy was born. She allowed his middle name to be hyphenated after me, and I was okay with that – at least my son had both my name and my father's name. And her dad and I had gotten along, although at first he wasn't thrilled his model daughter was dating and then married to a cowboy. She must have told him about my family's wealth because on our wedding day, Robert Barrett clapped me on the shoulder and said, "Welcome to the family, Micah. I know you'll take good care of my daughter and my grandchild."

"Yes, sir," I replied. "I will most certainly do that."

My parents graciously welcomed Ashley into our family, too. Despite the circumstances of our son's conception, they were excited to meet their grandchild. We stayed with my parents at the ranch through that first year of our marriage, my mother attempting to teach Ashley the running of a ranch household. My wife feigned interest, and I still give her credit for trying new things, but between life on the ranch and the pregnancy, she soon became more irritable. I tried, as the doctor said, to chalk it up to hormones, but then two years later, she told me she was leaving. Just announced it. No attempt to discuss her decision. No interest in marital counseling.

"I can't live like this, Micah," she said. "I'm not meant to be a rancher's wife. I love the spotlight. I love the cities. I miss traveling, I miss the attention and accolades."

I tried to reason with her, appeal to her spiritual nature. She shot that down, too.

"I've tolerated your return to Christianity and your obsession with prayer and going to church. I don't believe in anything other than what I can see, feel, touch. I believe in now, today. And today I want to go back to the life I had. It was exciting! It was fun! This," and she had swept her hand around our bedroom, in which our son was sleeping in his crib, "this is not fun. I'm not cut out for this type of life. So I'm leaving."

She signed over her custody rights and returned to modelling full-time. That was nearly three years ago. We've seen her once since then. She needed money. I gave it to her. I gave her a lot, and I told her I never wanted to see or hear from her again. Our son didn't recognize her then and she pretended not to know him. I had loved her, not deeply, although I tried. I tried to be the man God expected of me. Since returning to Christ, I wanted to love the mother of my child as the woman I married, the woman who was supposed to be my wife. Ashley rejected me, my son, my family, and my God, and I didn't want her just popping into our lives when she felt like it. Or when she needed, or wanted, money again. So, I gave her part of my trust fund, money left me by my grandfather. I believed that would keep her for decades. It should. By then, our son would be old enough to make his own decisions.

I've been evasive when Bobby has asked questions, which hasn't been often. He knows his mother is traveling the world for her job and I've said she will see him when she's done.

After seeing Hannah again at my parents' house, last night I began wondering if God led me through the heartache of divorce and kept the desire to date other women at bay because He ordained this reconnection.

What do I want, really? Most importantly, what does He want?

My phone rang and I glanced at the caller ID. I put Hannah's number in my cell phone's contact list after Mom gave it to me. My heart leaped seeing that number on the screen of my phone.

My heart hammered as I picked up the call.

"Hi. Thanks for calling me back."

I hoped my voice sounded steady in her ears. In mine, the words seemed wobbly.

"Yeah, no problem. I just wanted you to know I got your message. That was kind of you. Thank you."

"Are you busy tomorrow?" I asked bluntly.

"Well, I ...."

Dude, what are you doing?

But I pressed on.

"I'd like to meet you for coffee."

Quickly, I added, "To talk about my parents' anniversary event. I'd really like to know if there's anything I can do this week to help make it happen."

"I do this for a living, Micah. I assure you everything's under control."

Gee, dude, you sure know how to compliment a woman!

"No, I didn't mean I don't think you know what you're doing, I just wanted you to know I'm available to help, so if there's anything I can do ...."

She sighed and then said, "I'm sorry. I didn't mean to bite your head off. It's just ... in the past I've had family members, whether it's a wedding, a birthday party, an anniversary .... Well, let's just say their attitudes have been less than encouraging, and that their offers of help have sometimes come across as condescending. I'm sorry for taking your words the wrong way."

"I get it. I'm sorry you've had those experiences."

"You know the Lord tells us we are to be a light in this world, but I admit my faith doesn't shine well when I feel I'm being questioned on my abilities. I still can get defensive, and, again, I'm sorry. I assure you, I've listened to what your parents want, I've run ideas by them, and I've consulted with them the whole way these past six weeks."

"Yeah, they've told me, and they are appreciative of what you're doing. I am too. I just wanted you to know that."

A moment of silence passed and then a lightbulb went off in my head.

"Did I hear you say birthday parties?"

"Yes. I've done hundreds, both in Seattle and here since I came back."

"When was that, by the way?"

My question was genuine. Realizing yesterday that my parents and little sister knew Hannah returned to Highwood Hills but had kept that from me still left a wound. Would I have sought her out had I'd known?

Well, that's neither here nor there now.

Hannah responded to my question.

"Almost two years ago. I got tired of the big city, and I missed my family. Aunt Eileen fell and broke her hip, and my cousin needed some help with her. At first it was to be temporary, but then I fell in love again with the little town and surrounding area, the mountains, the green hillsides, the rivers and streams, the wildlife. I started getting some work and I decided to move back and be close to family and friends again."

"Well, that's great! I'm glad things are working out for you. And your aunt – how is she doing?"

"Very well actually. She and I garden together, vegetable and flowers, we feed the birds, and I help her with her community cat project. We've even taken in a few dogs and found new homes for them. And she works with some of the less feral cats, socialized them, tamed them, and works with a nearby cat rescue organization to get them adopted."

I laughed.

"Yeah, mom's mentioned about Eileen's little zoo."

"I enjoy helping her – she cares for God's creatures that others ignore. But it's a good thing we don't own as much land as your family does – I don't think she'd adopt out as many. Instead, she'd keep most of them!"

Hannah chuckled. I relished her laugh, the merriment, the joy. Ashley rarely laughed and most times when she did, it sounded fake.

For the millionth time during the past seven years, I thought, *Why, oh, why did I make such a stupid mistake and leave Hannah? I loved her, and I let my pride and selfishness get in the way.*

"So, you asked about birthday parties?"

Her question brought me back from my thoughts.

"Yeah, uh, Bobby's fifth birthday is a week after Thanksgiving. I know you have a lot on your plate with my parents' anniversary party on Saturday, but do you think you could squeeze in a boy's fifth birthday party?"

Silence.

I overstepped, asked too much of her.

"Well, I might be able to. Let's talk after Saturday. Give me a few thoughts and let me stew on them."

"How about coffee tomorrow?" I asked again.

"Micah, I have so much on my plate right now with your parents' party. I just don't know how I'd be able to ...."

"Just an hour. Again, perhaps you'll think of something I can help with for the folks' party."

Another moment of silence passed, and then I said, "I really do want to help. I've been gone for several months and I'd like to see how I might contribute to their special celebration."

"All right. Let me think about it and I'll plan to meet you tomorrow at ten. But just an hour – there are lots of small things still to do, and they add up. We only have a few days until their event."

"Great! I'll meet you at Amy's Buck'n'Brew tomorrow at ten."

Hannah

At ten o'clock the next morning, I found myself on the sidewalk just outside Amy's Buck'n'Brew. I took a deep breath before pulling open the door to the little coffee house.

I whispered a scripture I had chosen as my life verse: "I can do all things through Christ who gives me strength."

He's a client, just like any other client.

Then came the reasoning part of me.

Yeah, Hannah, you keep telling yourself that.

So I did. As I opened the door. As I stepped through the door. As I looked around the bistro-style coffee café.

He's a client.

I said it again as I caught his eye. And once more as he stood up from the table at the back of the shop.

I nearly had to whisper it aloud as he gave me that grand smile, the one that swept me off my feet from the first time we met when I was fifteen and kept my heart captivated all through high school. That dashing, winsome, delightful smile.

I walked toward Micah, and he met me partway.

"Good to see you, Hannah," he whispered. "Thanks for meeting me this morning."

Although I had seen him just yesterday, I had not allowed myself to drink in his appearance. I took that opportunity now, and what I saw before me almost made me gawk. His six-foot-two frame with broad shoulders, muscular arms, and burly chest filled out the button-down tan linen shirt he wore. He had certainly matured physically in

23

seven years! The ranch and rodeo work agreed with him. No wonder he had captured the eye and heart of a gorgeous model! I almost felt ashamed to stand near him. My five-foot-six-inch stature and non-voluptuous body seemed miniscule compared to the images of the five-foot-nine-inch, curved-in-the-right-places, movie-star-like model Ashley Bennett. I almost averted my eyes. Almost.

You are a child of God.

I stood taller.

You are an Esther.

I smiled at my former boyfriend, looked him in the eye, and held out my hand to shake his.

"Good to see you, too, Micah."

He did the unexpected. At least, unexpected to me. He hugged me.

Those arms. So strong, so warm. That chest. So broad, so comforting. That breath. So endearing. I nearly melted.

I returned Micah's embrace, and I closed my eyes.

This feels right, oh, so right!

Tears threatened to leak from the corners of my eyes. Had it really been seven years? Being held like this seemed like no time had passed.

He stepped away and I immediately felt cold. I wanted him to hold me again, but I couldn't say that.

I pasted on a smile and said, "So, have you ordered?"

"No, I was waiting for you. What would you like? My treat."

"No, no. I'll get my own. After all, this is a business meeting. Let me get yours. I can take it off my taxes."

Did I really say that?

Micah looked hurt. I tried to back pedal a bit.

"I mean, we can go Dutch if you'd rather."

"I'd rather buy your coffee. This, uh, meeting, was my idea after all. And I owe you so much more than a coffee."

Ah, guilt.

I shrugged.

"Sure, whatever. I'll wait for you at the table. I can get a bit more work done while you order. I'll take, uh, how about a, um..."

Oh, good grief, Hannah! You know what coffee you like! Spit it out, girl!

"Please order an Irish Cream latte for me."

Micah cracked a smile and said, "Still drinking those, are you?"

I gave him my I-don't-care-what-you-think smile.

"Yep. Still do. If it's not broke, don't fix it."

After slipping into the bench seat at the table Micah had chosen earlier, I removed my phone from the bamboo-woven purse I carried. The over-the-shoulder bag my cousin had brought back from her trip to Thailand last year was my favorite purse. *One day,* I thought for the thousandth time, *one day I'm going to take vacations like that.*

I should have done so while I was still in Seattle. The one trip to Hawaii and the adventurous excursion to Australia and New Zealand whetted my appetite for more such vacations, but the return to and subsequent residence in Montana set me back a few years. Living with Aunt Eileen saved money on living expenses, but building a business again took time. And energy. And money.

The opportunity to travel would come. Just not quickly.

I looked at my phone but I couldn't concentrate. I glanced at Micah standing at the counter. He looked at me. I darted my eyes back to my phone, pretending to read email.

How in the world is this going to work? Can I really plan a birthday bash for his boy? In just a few weeks?

He's a client, Hannah, nothing more.

Liar.

I tried to focus on the influx of emails. Skimming the inbox, my eyes captured one I'd missed yesterday. I could hardly believe my eyes. Nearly two years had passed since the sender's name was even in my purview. Dare I open it?

Before my fingers could tap the Open Mail icon, Micah's voice came from behind me.

"One Irish cream latte."

I nearly jumped from the booth.

"Sorry, I didn't mean to startle you."

He set the coffee cup in front of me and then slid into the seat across the table.

"Must be important."

I looked at him as he set his coffee mug on the table. He returned my gaze.

"The email. You were quite focused on your email."

"Nothing I can't deal with later."

I placed the cell phone into the bamboo purse. Micah noticed it.

"That's unique." He nodded at the bag. "Your purse."

"Emma brought it back from Thailand last year."

"Oh? What took her there?"

"Mission trip with the youth at church."

"How's she and your aunt doing?"

"Good. Emma's been dating this guy ... Well, that wouldn't interest you."

I sipped the liquid in my cup. My tongue lit like a fire in a hearth. I licked my stinging lips.

"Amy makes her hot drinks really hot. I should have warned you," Micah announced.

I glanced at him. He was looking at me with a concerned expression. Not something I wanted to see.

I don't need you pretending to look out for me, I screamed inwardly. *Been living without you for seven years.*

I kept those inner thoughts to myself.

"I've been here a few times. I should have known better."

"What makes you think I wouldn't be interested in what's happening in Emma's life?"

His question puzzled me.

"What?"

"You started to tell me about Emma and then you said I wouldn't be interested. What makes you think that?"

"Come on, Micah. You haven't been interested in me or my family for seven years. Maybe actually longer. Why would I think that's changed?"

He stared at me a moment and then looked away.

Okay, Hannah, that was cruel and spiteful. The man just bought you coffee and sat down.

"Hey, look, I'm sorry ...." I started.

"No, don't apologize. It's me who needs to apologize," he said. "But what you said isn't true. I do care about you and your family. I did back then and I do now."

I studied his face and tried to hide my surprise at his confession. Of course, though, I was cynical.

"Forgive me if I don't believe you."

Micah looked at me. I was taken aback by the remorse reflected in his eyes and his expression. He took a deep breath and then exhaled.

I am sorry, Hannah, truly sorry," he whispered. "In fact, I'm sorry for a lot of things."

I wouldn't let my guard down. The last thing I needed was to let him get under my skin ... and back into my heart.

I'm not going to go there again.

I decided to be done with it all, here and now.

"It was a long time ago, Micah. We've both moved on."

"I know what it must look like, my wild life on the road, Ashley, having a son..."

"It looks like you once had an amazing relationship with a gorgeous woman and now you share a beautiful boy."

"Well, some of that's true, but our relationship, our marriage, wasn't all that amazing, as you say. Truth is ..."

"Listen, Micah, let's leave the past in the past. You wanted to talk about your son's birthday. Tell me what you're thinking. About the party, that is."

His gaze stayed on me for a few seconds. Then he said, "Bobby turns five the first week of December. I want this birthday to be extra special. With his mom out of our lives, well, I just want him to know he's loved, that his aunt, his grandparents, his dad really love him."

My heart contracted. What pain that boy must feel to not have his mother around to show him that same type of love that Micah and his family obviously have for him. For a moment, I put myself in little Bobby's shoes. My own parents have been missing from my life for more than ten years. I still felt the pain from their absence. Bobby must experience that, too.

Micah's boy and I had a sad thing in common. At least Bobby still had his dad and grandparents. For a moment, I wondered about the other side of his family.

"What about Ashley's family? Are they still part of his life?"

Micah shook his head.

"My former father-in-law passed away and Ashely's mother moved to France before she and I split up. I think that's another reason she left – she wanted to spend more time in Europe, and though I was happy to let her go visit, the lure of that more luxurious life drew her back to the limelight. So she moved to France to live with her mother and return to modeling. Although I could understand her wanting to be with her mother for a time, I actually thought they'd come to the ranch together. I was wrong."

My heart softened.

"I'm sorry, Micah."

He gave me a brief smile.

"Thanks. My heart aches for Bobby, but truthfully, Ashley and I weren't compatible. Ranch living and following a rodeo circuit wasn't for her."

"Why did you marry her?"

My blunt outburst surprised even me.

"I'm sorry! It's none of my business ...." I began.

Micah waved his hand.

"It's okay. Honestly, I married her because of Bobby. Ashley was pregnant when we got married."

Surprise registered on my face, I'm sure, because Micah chuckled.

"Yeah. Most people don't know. She wasn't showing yet on our wedding day."

"I'd say not!"

Micah tilted his head, so I confessed.

"I saw some of the wedding pictures online."

A slight smile crooked his mouth.

"So you cyberstalked me?"

I blushed and looked away.

"It's okay. I cyberstalked you, too."

He grinned. I burst out laughing. After a moment of silence and another sip from my coffee cup, I prompted, "So, about this birthday party."

Micah

I realized I missed so much about Hannah, and her joyful laughter was one of the biggest. I basked in the sincerity she projected. Fakeness surrounded my ex-wife, and why I didn't notice that sooner ... or perhaps I did and just ignored it. I faked a lot of things, too, in those early days. I wished my younger self knew then what I came to know during the past five years. But that's what prodigals are – they are learners.

Laughter lacked in my life until I returned home. Ashley was playful and flirtatious, but she didn't laugh often, and rarely did I detect sincerity when she did laugh. I came to learn much of Ashley was simply pretense, an act, and I was traveling the same road. Until the prodigal returned home.

"So, is a baseball theme or a ranch theme?"

I studied Hannah's face after she posed the question, and I pondered a moment.

"Well, he's around ranch stuff all the time, but he hasn't expressed much interest in baseball yet."

"What are some things he does enjoy, besides the ranch and all that goes with it?"

"His first love is horses, and so I'm getting him his first pony," I told her.

A large, bright smile came to Hannah's face, and she bubbled with joy once again.

"Oh, he's going to love that, Micah! What a special gift!"

The merriment in her voice reflected in her eyes. Those eyes. Gemstone green. Twinkling. This woman was truly happy for my little boy. I knew at once this is the woman I should have married. I moved my hand across the table and clasped one of hers that surrounded the coffee cup she held.

"You amaze me," I said in a quiet tone.

She gave me a puzzled look.

"You're happy about something I plan to give another person."

Ashley was only happy when someone gave her something. And then I wondered, was she really happy even then? Did Ashley know about true happiness, true joy? How could she when she rejected Christ?

"Well, I still remember my first horse," Hannah said in a gentle voice. "I know the pleasure of not only receiving that gift, but the years of enjoyment I had with her. I'm sure Bobby will have a similar experience."

I smiled.

"No one forgets their first horse."

Or their first love, I guess.

Holding her hand awakened feelings long dormant. Like a wildflower in spring, my heart opened wide, and I knew the feeling of being in love began to sprout once again.

Hannah was a Christian woman. Why did I walk away from her?

Because I wasn't a Christian man. Not like now. And I still fall short. I immediately sent up a prayer of thanksgiving for God's tender mercies, for second chances. Second chances not only with Him and my faith, but a second chance with Hannah. If that's what this was.

Hannah didn't release my hand. I felt her fingers twitch. Was it nerves or was it a caress? I didn't move my hand. I simply looked at her.

Seven years had passed since I'd seen her. A more mature woman now sat in front of me. Her physical features captivated me, yes, but her heart, her gentleness, her kindness, radiated her suntanned face. I thought of Proverbs 31 – I often saw the noble characteristics written in that chapter reflected in my mother, but I now clearly saw them in Hannah: confidence, quiet strength, kindness, dignity, strong faith.

Charm is deceptive, and beauty is fleeting; but a woman who fears the LORD is to be praised. A woman of noble character who can find? She is worth far more than rubies.

Those verses from Proverbs 31 popped into my brain. In spite of her parents' untimely, unexpected deaths when she was fifteen and coming to leave with her grieving aunt and cousin, Hannah maintained that quiet strength and dignity. That's what drew me to her in the first place. I still saw that in eyes and on her face, but even more so after nearly a decade.

My hand felt warm in a delightful way. That feeling crept up my arm and spread through my body. I continued to gaze at her. Hannah possessed beauty even my model ex-wife did not. My thoughts traveled from the Old Testament book of Proverbs to the New Testament scripture where Peter talked about inward and outward beauty: "Clothe yourself with the beauty that comes from within, the unfading beauty of a gentle and quiet spirit which is so precious to God."

Ashley possessed outward beauty, even now, but the woman sitting across from me is the kind talked about in Proverbs and by the Apostle Peter. Outward beauty was more important to me when I was twenty, but later I realized as Solomon stated in many of his proverbs, that type of beauty is vain. I was vain. I was selfish. I was prideful. And I hurt this beautiful woman who possesses what's important to God ... because God was, and is, important to her.

I uttered a loud, but inaudible cry, for forgiveness, and I asked the Lord, if it was His will, to give me a second chance with Hannah. My heart experienced a deep cleansing much like when I asked for God's forgiveness of my prodigal ways and His help in following Him again. My mind and soul experienced peace as I acknowledged to God, and to myself, deep into the depths of my being that I was again falling in love with Hannah Anne Donovan. Or as the inaudible Voice whispered, "You never stopped loving her."

"Micah, are you okay?"

Hannah's whispered question brought me out of my deep reflection. I smiled.

"Yeah. Just having a little inward conversation with the Lord."

"Oh. I have those sometimes, too."

"I'm sure you do. He wants that from His children."

She nodded and replied softly, "And His children need that connection with their Father."

"Hannah, I ..."

I paused and took a deep breath. As I exhaled, I squeezed her hand.

"Do you think ... would you want ... could we, I mean I would like ..."

Her cell phone rang, and I withdrew my hand from hers.

Hannah

When my cell phone jingled the tune of *Hark! The Herald Angels Sing*, I jumped in my seat. Micah withdrew his hand as if he'd been burned by a hot flame. He sat back against the bench, and I glanced at the caller ID.

"It's the caterer," I informed him.

I slid from the wooden seat and wandered to the other side of the café before answering.

"Hi, Patrick. I still plan to come by in a few hours ..."

His next words made my heart stop.

"My shrimp shipment's been delayed. It won't arrive until Saturday morning. We need to rethink the shrimp cocktail. The sooner you can get here the better so we can select something else."

"That's the one item they both want. We can't choose something else."

"No shrimp, no shrimp cocktail. I can't make the little buggars simply show up!"

"Can you order from a different company?"

"Not this late in the game. I placed the order with my supplier a month ago."

"Well, you need a different supplier."

I heard his exasperated sigh.

"Hannah, your sarcasm doesn't help. When can you get here?"

I glanced toward Micah. He was watching me. I turned my back toward him and whispered into the phone, "Twenty minutes."

I clicked off and then I took a deep breath to steady my nerves. How could this happen? Where could I find enough shrimp for eighty-five shrimp cocktails on such short notice?

"Everything okay?"

Micah's deep voice caused me to whirl around with an "Oh!"

I tried not to tremble.

His parents, his entire family, and Micah himself are going to hate me, my brain screamed. *My career as an event planner in this area, the entire region most likely, will be drained like the swimming pool in the town's park at the end of summer.*

I plastered a smile on my face.

"Know any good shrimp suppliers?"

Micah's face scrunched. I sighed and then I placed my hand on his arm and led him to a small alcove near the hallway to the restrooms.

"What's going on, Hannah?"

I took another deep breath, glanced around to make sure no one was in earshot, and then I exhaled once again.

"The shrimp for the shrimp cocktails for your parents' party won't be here in time for Patrick, the caterer, to get the appetizers ready. He wants me to make a different selection."

"My parents love shrimp cocktail."

I nodded.

"I know that. I told Patrick it's non-negotiable. But he says it's impossible because the shipment is delayed until Saturday morning."

"The party doesn't start until four o'clock."

"Yeah, but there's all the other food. Your parents ordered a lot, Micah. I mean enough to feed your father's Navy shipmates back in the day."

I felt relief when Micah smiled. At least my attempt at a small joke struck him as humorous. However, that didn't help our situation.

"How much extra help does this Patrick need on Saturday morning?"

"What?"

"How many people would it take to get those shrimp cocktails made? This is my parents' party and I'm willing to help."

I put my hands on my hips.

"What do you know about making shrimp cocktails?"

"Enough. I hung out with lots of celebrities and went to enough swanky galas. I'm not just a bronc rider and rancher, you know."

This time I smiled.

"I'm not really sure I want to know, but okay. How about this? Why don't you come with me to meet Patrick and talk with him? But I'm sure he'll need more help than one bronc rider and rancher to get those appetizers created and ready on time."

Micah grinned.

"I know some people."

I grinned back.

"I do, too."

"And wherever two or three are gathered ..."

I continued to grin at him as I responded, "I don't think that verse refers to creating shrimp cocktails."

"No, but nothing says we can't pray over them ... and the shipment."

I shook my head and then said, "No, no it doesn't. Since when did you learn to quote so much Scripture?"

His grin faded and he looked away. I reached out my hand and placed it on his arm.

"I'm sorry, Micah. That was cruel, and I didn't mean ...."

He looked at me solemnly.

"No, you're right. I wasn't much of a Christian back then. I played the part well in public, but my heart was full of pride and selfishness."

His hand enclosed mine and he looked deeply into my eyes.

"That's what I've been waiting for a good time to talk with you about. I want to sincerely apologize, Hannah. I hurt you and I'm sorry. I made a lot of bad choices back then. I'm a prodigal that's returned to

God and to my family. I know what I did may be unforgivable, but I want you to know I'm sincerely sorry."

Gazing back at him, I saw genuine remorse in his eyes. Those eyes that stole my heart a decade ago. Those eyes that made me feel like the most special girl in the world. Those eyes who danced with laughter and burned with desire. Those eyes that held my gaze as he held my hand during our dates. Those eyes that flashed with anger when I begged him to not break up our relationship. Those eyes that haunted me for seven years even though I tried to put them, and him, out of my mind and my heart.

"I forgive you," I whispered.

He embraced me and I felt the burden he'd been carrying fall away. My resentment and anger, like baggage a traveler carries, dropped from me as well. We stood for several minutes holding onto one another. A man walked by and remarked with a sneer, "Oh, go get a room!"

I stepped away from Micah and gave him an embarrassed smile.

"So, do you want to go meet with a chef?"

I made him laugh again and my heart swelled with joy. I grinned widely.

We walked toward the door, and Micah asked, "How about afterward we go for a short drive and see the colors? They seem to have held on longer this year."

I nodded and then I responded, "They have. October was simply spectacular, I thought, and now here we are in early November, with many of the trees still displaying their colorful leaves."

Micah held the glass door open for me. I felt my heart skip a beat. Montana men, especially cowboys, seem to have that instinct for old-time chivalry. I've come to greatly appreciate that.

"So how about it? Meet the chef, convince him me and my buddies can handle whipping together the shrimp cocktails and then go and enjoy the glory of late autumn? Maybe even take a short trail walk."

He stopped and looked at me. I chewed my lower lip. *Still so much to do,* my brain argued.

"I'm not sure, Micah. I still need to stop at the florist and I have an appointment with my cousin to meet with the woman supplying the decorations. Tomorrow I'm supposed to meet with your parents ...."

He placed gentle hands on my shoulders.

"You're carrying a big load. Let me help. Jill and I are back now from the rodeo, and we can help. I'm going to recruit her for shrimp duty, too, by the way."

I smiled.

"We have to get Patrick to agree first. And if we do, I'll ask Aunt Eileen and my cousin Emma to help."

"So, let's go put out this small fire and then go enjoy some time in God's creation. I'll make sure you're back in time to meet the florist. You need a break, even just a short one."

"This is my work, Micah, my job. The most critical time is the last week leading up to the event. You'll find this out when we put together Bobby's birthday party."

His eyes lit up.

"So you'll do it?"

I gave him a brief smile and nodded.

"He deserves a special birthday, and so yes, after your parents' anniversary party, I'll start on Bobby's party."

Micah wrapped me in his strong, warm arms and whispered, "Thank you."

As I stood there being held by the man who captured my heart nearly a decade ago, images of embraces past flashed through my mind. Picnics along the river. Dances at school. Kisses in the moonlight. Horse rides on the ranch and then embracing under the trees in the woodlands.

I relished those affections and the one I currently experienced. His masculine, outdoorsy smell tantalized my nose. I took a deep yet quiet breath, absorbing more of his scent. I closed my eyes. Another sensation tickled my insides, an emotion that laid dormant for more than half a decade. Simultaneously, we pulled each other closer, our bodies melting into one another. His lips lay close to my left ear, and his breath teased me.

"I love holding you like this." Micah whispered.

My eyes popped open.

What are we doing?

I stepped away. Micah's eyes opened and he looked at me, as if in a daze.

"I think we'd better go see the chef," I said.

I took two more steps away from him.

"I drive that Toyota 4-Runner you saw the other day," I said, pointing to my vehicle parked two places down from the coffee house.

"Hannah ..."

"Micah, please. This ... this is all too much."

He nodded.

"Just follow me to Patrick's catering office," I said. "It's on the corner of Bell and Spruce, behind the Mountain Oasis Restaurant."

"Okay. I drive a navy-blue Jeep Gladiator. It's parked across the street."

"I'll meet you at Patrick's office shortly."

I began to walk toward my vehicle and then decided to say something. I turned and faced Micah.

"I don't think we should take that drive or walk, not just yet. I feel, um, it's been a long time and though I believe we ... we have feelings for each other, I think we need to slow down a bit."

Micah nodded.

"You're right. I apologize for overstepping. We can still take a bit of time for an outing. I, uh, I promise to stay an arm's length away and not tempt either of us. You're correct, Hannah – I do have feelings for you, stronger than I imagined."

"I feel the same way," I confessed. "But I have your parents' anniversary party to concentrate on. I'll see you at Patrick's."

I turned away and took two quick breaths.

Please, Lord, help me. Help us. I can't take another broken heart.

Micah

Hannah and I met with the caterer and assured him that we and our friends and family could learn quickly to put together shrimp cocktails Saturday morning. Afterward, we drove from the valley to a local trailhead. We chatted about our lives during the past seven years, her time attending college and then later working in Seattle, her enjoyment of event planning, her reasons for returning to Highwood Hills, which primarily involved the health of her aunt, and her desire to serve others through her career. I let her know about my years on the rodeo circuit, missing my family and the central Montana landscape. I purposefully left out time spent with Ashley, only saying the best part of my marriage was the son we shared.

I elaborated more about Bobby and praised his wit and intelligence. I talked about his love for animals and his desire to either be a rancher like his dad and grandad or to become an astronaut. I told her about our visit to Kennedy Space Center, the Florida Keys and deep-sea fishing, and all the six-toed cats we met when we visited Hemmingway's Home in the Keys.

"Bobby loves cats. And horses. All animals, really," I told Hannah. "Not sure where he gets that from."

She chuckled.

"His dad. His grandmother. His grandfather. His aunt. Animals are in the Hanson genes."

I grinned.

"My mother's only been a Hanson for about 40 years."

"Well, I seem to recall her sharing stories about growing up on a farm in Idaho and having a lot of animals there. In fact, didn't she and her siblings have a tortoise?"

I laughed.

"How did you remember that? I had completely forgotten!"

Hannah shrugged and then said, "I likely remember because it was so unusual. Like my Aunt Eileen and her armadillo."

I laughed again, louder this time. Another story I'd forgotten.

"You remember some of the strangest things. I'm amazed at the things from a decade ago that you remember and I've forgotten. Probably from being thrown on my head so much."

We laughed.

I turned the Jeep Gladiator off the main highway and onto the gravel road that led to the foothills of the Highwood Mountains. The late autumn sunshine filtered through the truck cab, adding natural light and heat to the inside of the pickup.

"Mom says there still may be chokecherries on some of the bushes near the Jewel River, and that there may be some trout in the water yet," I said. "I'd like to get Bobby up here if there are any fish. We can pick some chokecherries and check out the river pools."

"Remember, I can't be gone too long. I am still working."

I glanced at Hannah. I knew the timing wasn't the best with my parents' anniversary party closing in, but I also knew we wouldn't have many autumn days like this. I returned my eyes to the roadway. Leaves remained on most of the aspen and tamarack trees, and a painted canvas of gold and red mixed with green from pine and juniper welcomed us to the lower hillsides of the towering Highwood Mountain Range. Sprinkled with snow like powdered sugar atop a batch of brownies, the mountains for which our community was named rose eight to ten thousand feet above the valley.

"I'll have you back within the hour," I promised her. "We just don't get many November days like this, and I heard next week might bring the first significant snowfall."

"I heard that too. At least Saturday's forecast remains autumn-like, just a bit cooler," she said.

A few moments later, I pulled the truck into a parking area next to the Jewel River trailhead. I set the vehicle in 'park' and shut off the engine.

"If we're going to pick chokecherries, what will we put them in?"

I smiled at Hannah's question and reached behind the driver's seat. I pulled out a blue and white ice cream bucket.

"I never leave home without it," I told Hannah. "Raspberries, strawberries, huckleberries, currants, chokecherries ... If I'm out and I see 'em, I take some home."

"The huckleberries were excellent this year! Aunt Eileen was so excited!"

"Okay, now I'm getting hungry again. Your aunt's huckleberry pie is even better than my mother's. But please don't let her I know I said that!"

Hannah chuckled and responded, "Why not? Your mother has said the same to my aunt."

She opened the passenger's side door.

"Let's go find some chokecherries and fish!"

I pulled a can of bear spray from the glovebox. Hannah looked at me, a puzzled expression on her face.

"Usually this time of year, the bears are going into hibernation, but with the long-lasting autumn, I'm assuming that's not the case this year," I explained. "I don't want to take a chance we might encounter one on the trail."

Hannah nodded and said, "Good idea. I didn't think about that since it is November."

FIFTEEN MINUTES LATER, we each stood by a chokecherry bush near the river's edge, the plastic pail between us. We picked and we talked. We laughed and we shared. When Hannah told me about her final year in Seattle and the half-crazed coworker who harassed her, heat crawled up the back of my neck.

"Did he get fired? He should have been!"

"That's the time Aunt Eileen broke her hip and Emma asked if I could come and help," she responded. "I thought time away would settle things and then when I had the opportunity to move back and return to the office, I decided not to. I opened my own business and so that's what I've been doing the past eighteen months."

"I'm surprised we didn't run into each other. I mean, I've been gone off and on, but I spent quite a bit of time at the ranch and around Highwood Hills."

"I was careful where I went and when I went," she murmured.

I looked at her. She continued to look at the fruit on the tree.

"You avoided me."

She nodded and didn't speak.

"Well, mom and dad didn't tell me they hired you as their party planner. All they said was that it's 'under control.'"

"Well, it was, and it is," she responded.

"Mom told me about the other events you've planned and how impressed she is with your work."

"Your mom is a kind woman."

I smiled.

"That she is."

I glanced at Hannah.

"I know several kind women."

She looked at me and our eyes locked.

"You know several women."

I realized that remark Hannah made came from the hurt and mistrust she still felt. She may have said she'd forgiven me, but I knew first-hand forgiveness was something a person had to do daily, no, actually each moment, until one day, the words became truth.

I chose to simply agree with her – to some degree.

"That used to be true. Now my life is focused on family and close friends."

"I'm sorry, Micah, I didn't mean to be cruel."

I smiled.

"Of course you did. And I don't blame you. I know forgiveness takes time – you felt betrayed, and I'm to blame for that. I hurt you, and I take responsibility for that."

I returned to picking chokecherries. A few moments ticked by and then Hannah said, "I'm glad your parents didn't say anything. Waiting until the last minute was for the best."

"Why's that?"

"To avoid awkward moments like we've had."

I looked at her, and she looked at me. Hannah continued in a low voice, "I was preparing myself to see you at the party, maybe even at the upcoming final check meeting. I planned to be poised and composed. Didn't turn out that way."

She took a deep breath and looked at the tree again. She ran her fingers over one of the branches and whispered, "I cried practically all the way to town the other day, after seeing you and Jill at your parents' house. I wasn't ready to see you yet."

I reached over and clasped my hand around hers, gave it a squeeze, and said in a low tone, "I'm sorry I caused you so much pain, then and now."

She looked at me, then at our clasped hands, and then back at me.

"You broke my heart, Micah," she whispered.

I bit my lip and looked up at the sky. I silently asked for guidance.

A moment later, I looked back at her and said, "I know. Believe me, I know. I turned my back on nearly everything I knew was true and beautiful. I think God protected you from further hurt, and I'm grateful He did. You wouldn't have lasted following me around. I've repented for my ways and returned to my family and to the Lord. I'm a very different person than I was when we were eighteen, when I was twenty and twenty-one. What happened with Ashley, having a son and caring for him, well, all of that brought me to my senses. Now that I'm home again and I have Bobby to raise, I understand how sin took over my life. I understand I let the devil drive. and I never intend to let that happen again. By God's grace."

We stared at one another for a moment. I hoped my face and my words showed my sincerity. I gave everything to the Lord at that moment with the thought of *Thy will be done.*

Hannah's hand squeezed mine.

"I really like this Micah John Hanson." She smiled and stated with conviction, "In fact, I really love this Micah John Hanson."

Her emerald eyes danced, and I saw that truth reflected. I brought her hand to my lips and kissed her knuckles gently. Everything inside of me wanted to draw her into my arms, but I suppressed that desire and simply looked into her eyes.

"I love you, too, Hannah."

I nearly choked with emotion but through the Spirit's miraculous work, each word spilled forth tenderly, sincerely, and with clarity. Her beautiful smile radiated on her face and then she said, "I hate to end this lovely morning, but I really need to get back to town."

I kissed her hand again and responded, "We have time, all the time we need, to spend together. We have parties coming up and holidays, too. We'll get to know each other all over again, just as we've started doing today. Let's go on a horseback ride when you come to the house tomorrow. Can you pencil me in for a few hours tomorrow?"

Her smile continued to touch my heart.

"I think, for you, I'll use pen."

I laughed, feeling as free and uplifted as an eagle in flight. I squeezed her hand again and then let go, saying, "Why don't you head back to the truck with the chokecherries and I'll jog upstream a short way to find that pool where the trout might be? I'll meet you at the parking lot."

I gave her the keys to the Gladiator.

"In case you need them."

"I'll pick a few more chokecherries. We'll have enough for more jelly for my aunt and your mom. Then I'll head down."

I nodded and then began to trot up the trail. Although it had been more than a year since I'd been here, the area began to feel more familiar. Another one thousand feet, and there it was, the bend in the trail with a short path toward the river. Among a covering of willows and grasses, I found the pool of the river at which dad and I had fished in previous years. I studied the water but saw no fish. I waited another moment. Still nothing. I glanced around and noticed some mud where likely some wildlife and water birds had played, gotten drinks, and took shelter. Within the dirt and mire I saw tracks. First a coyote. Then a few deer. And then – oh boy! Not quite what I wanted to see. And they were fresh. Likely made earlier this morning.

I took several steps to return to the main trail. Then I saw her. A mama black bear with two cubs-of-the-year. Thankfully, their backs were toward me, and they weren't grizzlies. But they were a family, a mom with young. I backed up slowly and unhooked the bear spray from my belt. The click made the mother bear turn. I stopped. Bears have poor eyesight but have great hearing. One of the babies turned my way as well. It gave a squeal. Mama bear rose on her hind legs and sniffed the air. I took two more steps back. The second cub turned my way. I froze. The mother bear continued to sniff, and I continued to hold my place.

My heart hammered in my chest and my palms grew sweaty. The cubs grew restless, bouncing on their paws. Mama bear dropped to the ground and swatted her youngsters, driving them to the nearest pine tree. Each cub bawled with each cuff from their mom. I took the opportunity to pull the can of bear spray from the holster and to take several brisk backward steps. The female bear must have heard leaves crunch under my shoes for she snorted and whirled back around to face me. I unlocked the trigger mechanism on the can while taking a few more steps backward. My left shoe caught on a branch and I fell onto my back. The can of bear spray slipped from my hand.

The bear roared and again stood on her hind legs and sniffed the air. She must have caught my scent because she dropped on all fours, roared again, this time as loud as I'd imagine a grizzly sounding and certainly as protective of her young.

The mother bear rushed toward me. My heart raced to my throat yet I still yelled, "Hannah! Get to the truck NOW!"

I reached for the bear spray as the female bruin charged.

Hannah

I heard Micah yell but couldn't quite make out the words. From my position part-way to the parking lot, I stopped. I listened a mere few seconds and then I heard more yelling. I also heard another noise, like grunts and growls. The hair on my neck and arms rose.

No, can't be.

Then I heard a scream of pain.

Micah!

I left the bucket of chokecherries along the side of the trail, and I ran back up the dirt path toward the sounds of more grunts, growls, and groanings. I found Micah lying on the ground, blood running along the left side of his leg.

"Micah!"

"Stay back, Hannah! Bears!"

Bears? More than one?

I looked straight ahead and saw two young black bears scurrying down a pine tree and what was likely their mother about fifty yards ahead. I looked at Micah again and saw his right hand holding the can of bear spray. I walked steadily toward him, keeping my eyes cast downward but also raising them now and then to see what the bears were doing. The mother was moving side-to-side, grunting, while her babies ran to get behind her.

"Give me the spray, Micah," I said in low yet commanding voice.

"You need to get back to the truck."

"Stop arguing. Hand me the spray can."

He raised his right hand slightly. I remembered that a bear's eyesight was poor so I prayed the mama bear didn't notice the motion. I also prayed she didn't see my arm reach down toward Micah and latch onto the can.

"How bad are you hurt?" I whispered.

"She bit my thigh. I don't think she got an artery, but still ..."

The mother growled and shook her head.

"Guess she heard us," I said in a low voice.

I took two steps forward. The bear grunted again and swayed.

"Hannah..."

"Shh."

I took two more steps forward and extended my left leg, sliding my right leg afterward. I took a defensive stance and now stood between Micah and the bear. I readied the spray can.

"Hannah!"

The bear roared and charged. I raised my arms outward and roared back. The bear skidded to a stop. She appeared confused. I roared again and she scampered backward. I took the moment to check the wind. If she charged again, I could release the spray and not risk covering myself instead of her.

She *woofed* in a low voice. I glanced behind her to see the cubs scamper back several feet. Mama retreated a few steps and I took the opportunity to roar again and rush toward her.

"Hannah! No!"

Micah's voice made Mama Bear dig in her protective instincts and she raced toward me. I prepared the pepper spray and when she was within range, I pushed the nozzle. The bear's face hit the mist and she howled in pain. She stopped her advance, howled again, and turned and raced toward her cubs. The mama bear huffed and snorted, the pepper likely in her eyes and nose, and she and her cubs ran swiftly into the woods, off the trail.

I stood for a moment, the adrenaline coursing through me. I watched the wooded area for several seconds. I didn't want to turn my back on the bruin family just yet.

"Hannah."

Micah's beleaguered voice reached me. I backed up slowly, eyes still on the place where the bears disappeared. When I reached him, Micah raised his left arm and enclosed his hand around my forearm.

"I'm bleeding."

That reminder made me whip my eyes from the forest and onto his face and then down to his leg. The wound was deep and blood spewed out from his thigh. I dropped down and grabbed his left arm, putting it across my shoulders.

"On the count of three," I said. "One, two, three!"

Micah's right leg bore a lot of weight, which helped me get him off the ground. We stood still for a few seconds.

"You okay?" he asked in a whisper.

I nodded.

"She got the pepper spray. The wind worked in our favor."

I took a step.

"Can you help me get you to the truck?"

Micah nodded. We took another step together. He winced.

"I'm not leaving you on the trail. Work with me, Micah."

"Trying."

We took two more steps, and he grimaced.

"We can't stay here. Mama may come back," I whispered.

"I know."

We took several more steps, Micah moaning low. I knew the pain must be horrendous so I kept encouraging him. After nearly fifteen minutes, we arrived at the truck. I lowered the tailgate and he leaned against it.

"First aid kit?"

"Behind the driver's seat," he responded.

I ran to the front of the Gladiator and I pulled out my phone.

Please! We need service!

Two bars registered and I gave a quick prayer of thanks. I pushed 9-1-1 and an operator answered.

"9-1-1, what's your emergency?"

"My boy ... my friend and I are at the Jewel River Trailhead. He's been bitten by a black bear and we need emergency help immediately. I have a first aid kit and after I patch him up, I'll be driving toward Highwood Hills ...."

"Wait a moment please, ma'am. A bear attack? Are you sure?"

"Black bear. Mom with cubs. Please, send an ambulance to meet us. We'll be in a dark blue Jeep Gladiator."

"Ma'am, please stay on the line."

"I'll leave the line open, but I've got to stop the bleeding."

I grabbed the first aid kit and raced back to Micah. His eyes were closing.

"Micah, Micah! I know you're in pain, but you've got to stay awake."

"Ma'am," said the operator.

"I'm here."

I looked closely at Micah's wounds.

"He has puncture marks, four of them, likely from the bear's teeth, on his left leg."

"Okay. You folks stay with me. I have an ambulance enroute. What highway are you near?"

I looked at Micah.

"Fifty-four."

His voice sounded weak. I looked into his eyes.

"Stay with me, Micah. I'll get you bandaged up and we'll get to a hospital."

I took gauze from the first aid kit and began to wind it around his left leg. Silently I prayed.

Father, help us. Lord, we need you, Micah needs you. Please send your angels to keep us and please stop the bleeding. Let him live, Lord, please, let him live.

Micah

I opened my eyes to a white ceiling with florescent lights. I blinked several times, trying to adjust to this new setting.

Hospital.

I could see two white walls and a curtain separated me from what I figured was another patient area, and I assumed another white wall was behind the headboard of the bed.

A small, single bed.

Yep, hospital.

I glanced around after my eyes adjusted. My dad sat in a chair several feet away, his head on his chest. How long he'd been there, I didn't know. I didn't know how long I was out – there was no clock on the wall. A few windows were part of the wall on my left. Blackness left little to be seen except for a few streetlamps. I reached to my left, hoping to find an end table and my cell phone. I moved slightly and pain shot from my knee to my hip.

"AWW!"

Dad jumped from his chair and was at my side in a heartbeat.

"Micah!"

"Hey, Dad. Sorry to wake you."

"No, no, not a problem. I was just dozing."

"What time is it?"

"About seven in the evening."

"Oh, man!"

I tried sitting up, but the pain again hit hard and I slipped back onto the pillows.

"Let's see if I can figure this out."

Dad took a remote control from the side of the bed. He pressed a button and the back of the bed began to rise, taking my body with it.

"Thanks, Dad. That's great."

"You sure? I think I have the hang of this thing ..."

I gave him a brief smile.

"No, this is good, just right."

I sighed.

"So, bring me up to speed. What happened after Hannah got me to the truck?"

"Well, the ambulance met you two half-way to town. I guess that girl knows how fast your Gladiator can go."

Dad chuckled.

"Is it still in one piece?"

"Yes, it actually is."

"And after the ambulance?"

"You went into surgery right away and have been given some antibiotics. The surgeon stopped the bleeding and repaired the muscles. He says you'll be walking again in about a week."

"A week?! No, I gotta do better than that."

"Now, son, your mother and I have talked, and ..."

"You are not postponing your party."

The door to the room opened and closed and my mother pulled the curtain back.

"We are, and we'll hear nothing more about it. You need to heal, Micah."

"I will heal. Therapy, exercise, whatever it takes."

"Rest, rest is what it takes," my mother said.

"Mom ...."

She held up one hand as she passed a coffee cup from the other to my father.

"Micah John Hanson, there is no discussion on this matter. Your health is top priority."

"I am healthy. I just need some recovery time. I'll stay here a few days, get to walking, have therapy, then have physical therapists come out to the house. You'll see – I'll be dancing in no time."

"Well, one of those dances better be with me, cowboy."

I turned to see Hannah standing near the curtain. Her half-smile made me smile.

"Hannah!"

I tried to sit up but crashed when the pain stabbed like a knife in my thigh.

"Son, sit back."

"Listen to your parents. As always, they are wise."

"Hannah, don't let them cancel the party."

"Not cancel, just postpone."

"Til when? There's Thanksgiving, then Bobby's birthday, then Christmas and New Years. There's no other time."

"We could have a New Year's Eve party and the anniversary party together," Mom suggested. "Or the anniversary and Bobby's birthday party at the same time."

"Mom, there is no need to postpone. I will be walking just fine, I promise."

I watched their faces. Mom looked at Dad and he at her. They both gazed at Hannah and she glanced at me.

"What do you think, Hannah?" Dad asked.

"It's totally up to you as a family. We are all set. Everything is in place for Saturday. Perhaps Micah can come in a wheelchair ..."

"Uh, uh. This cowboy rides horses, not wheelchairs."

I reached for Hannah. She walked to the right side of the bed. I enclosed my hand around hers and said sincerely and tenderly, "Thank you. Thank you for saving my life."

She smiled and leaned down. She kissed my cheek gently but fire radiated through me.

"You're welcome. And I'll save you a dance."

I heard the door to the hospital room open and close.

I smiled and said, "That gives me motivation to recover. Not only will I walk into that resort, but I'll be dancing with this wonderful lady, thank you very much."

A doctor stepped in. He looked at me and said, "Well, then, we'd better get you set up for physical therapy. How about we start tonight?"

Hannah

I felt as though I lived in the center of a tornado, having that encounter with Mama Bear, helping Micah get to the Jeep, binding his bleeding wounds, and driving toward town. The ambulance met us partway and I followed it the hospital's ER. And then worrying all night, texting him and his mother, making sure he was all right. Then, earlier today, driving out to the JBarN and finalizing everything and hanging out with the family, including little Bobby. Now I was back on track and back in town. My first visit was Chloe's floral shop and then later today, checking in again with Patrick and with Michael, the resort manager.

Saturday was fast approaching, Thankfully, my cousin, Emma, took charge of the decorations in order to take some tasks off my hands. The bear incident rattled me. I recited several Bible verses regarding fear and anxiety, including "I can do all things through Christ who strengthens me."

My back straight and my resolve restored, I stepped into the flower shop. Chloe's large smile greeted me, and another strong sense of calm enveloped me.

"Things are going wonderfully on this end," she beamed. "I can't wait to show you how they look!"

She took my hand and led me to the back room. Three crystalline vases with burnt-orange mums, white daisies, and yellow day lilies lined like soldiers on the cutting table. Sprigs of baby's breath and green cedar added more color to glass flower holdings. Small orange and white pumpkins and miniature green and yellow gourds surrounded each arrangement. A white paper doily lay underneath the arrangements and a tan card with yellow scripted words that said either "Faith," "Family," "Love," or "Thankful" completed each setting.

Simple yet elegant.

I smiled.

"Chloe, the Hansons are going to love this! What a festive fall theme! The lilies and daisies are just what they asked for. And you've captured the tone of what they want this night to reflect – family, faith, love, and gratitude. Well done!"

My friend smiled.

"I'm so glad you like it. I thought about adding another small flower to the bouquet but I didn't want to overdo. I know you'd need to get their approval since we didn't plan any other flowers. I think the arrangements need a bit more 'posh.' What do you think they might like?"

"How about some sprigs of tan wheat grass? It would reflect the ranch and not draw attention away from the color of the flowers."

Her eyes lit up and she said, "I like that idea! Would you ask them?"

"Of course. I'll text them. Do you have anything we could use as a sample?"

I could see her thinking, and then, with a smile, she snapped her fingers.

"Yes! Left over from a wedding I did last month. Grasses keep when taken care of. Let me get some and you can take a picture of it."

She bounded to the back flower room directly behind the workstation, and I texted Nadine Hanson with the idea. As Chloe returned, my phone dinged and I saw a thumbs-up emoji and a heart. I smiled at Chloe.

"Mrs. Hanson approves of adding another element. Let's see what you got."

I looked on the table where Chloe had placed three stalks of tan wheat grass, its wispy plumage gracing the ends. She also set out three shoots of darker rye grass, with shades of plum and mahogany gracing the stalks.

"I think the lighter compliments best," I said.

"Shall we do a vase of each and see what Mrs. Hanson says?"

"Good idea."

After Chloe placed one piece of wheat grass into a flower vase and one stem of the rye grass into another, I took a photo of the arrangements side-by-side. I texted the picture to Mrs. Hanson and asked, "Which one?"

As we awaited her response, Chloe asked, "How is Micah doing? I heard about the bear encounter."

"He's recovering. It was quite frightening, really."

"What were you doing out there with him anyway? That guy ripped your heart apart."

"Well, he asked for forgiveness. He's quite remorseful, and he's back on track in his faith. Maybe even more than me."

Chloe placed her hands on her hips.

"Just because a guy says he's sorry doesn't mean two cents."

"I have to follow what God wants, not what I want. And, to tell you the truth, since I have finally, fully forgiven him, I feel so much more at peace. In fact, I've discovered I really do love him."

Hands still on her hips, Chloe tossed her head.

"Well, of course! You always have. You've rarely dated and you've gone out of your way to avoid him since you moved back. You used to always shop at Natalie and John's Western and Casual Clothing but you haven't set foot in there since you came back to Highwood Hills."

I shrugged.

"I haven't needed new clothes. I had a lot in Seattle that came with me."

"And you really patched him up after the bear attack?"

"I know first aid – required for an event planner. One never knows if a client or guest will fall or have a heart attack."

"Or be bitten by a black bear. And Game and Fish is going to let her roam?"

"She was defending her cubs. She bit Micah's thigh and left – well, after a little coaxing from me and a can of bear spray."

"Yeah, and what kind of a person pulls stunt like that? What were you thinking, Hannah?"

"You sound like my aunt. It could have been much worse but it wasn't."

"You never said why you were with him. Are you two back together?"

My phone blipped.

"Saved by the text," Chloe commented.

I looked at my phone.

TAN WHEAT GRASS.

I looked at Chloe and said, "Tan wheat grass it is. Mrs. Hanson and I agree."

"I hope she agrees on the wedding dress you pick out."

Chloe scooped up the grass samples.

I tried to reprimand her, saying, "Chloe! There's no wedding."

"Oh, but there will be, I'm sure, and if I'm not the florist for your wedding, I'll put you on Santa's naughty list!"

She sashayed to the back room, and I shook my head.

"We're just getting to know each other again, so no wedding, you hear me?"

Her laughter rang out from the back room.

Micah

I lay on my right side on the couch in the living room. Bobby sat across from me on the floor. A checkerboard with red and black playing pieces on the coffee table separated us.

"Dad, it's your move."

"Oh, sorry, son. I got distracted."

I studied the board again.

"Thinkin' about the bear?"

"Kind of hard not to. I was pretty lucky."

"Yah. She coulda killed ya."

My son is pretty bright. Sometimes I wish he wasn't.

"Bobby ..."

"Dad, why is that my name?"

I looked at him, puzzled.

"Your name? What do you mean, son?"

"Why do people call me 'Bobby?'"

"Because your first name is 'Robert.' Lots of boys named 'Robert' are called 'Bobby.'"

"Yeah, but ..."

I noticed his hesitation.

"But what?"

"Why am I named 'Robert?' I thought my first name would be yours or grandpa's. But those are my middle names. I'm just wondering why ... why isn't my first name 'Micah' and my middle name 'John,' like you?"

His questions took me aback. He didn't know his maternal grandfather any more than he knew his mother. How could I explain to a four-year-old-going-on-five that one of the conditions his mother gave me for giving birth to him and staying around was that our son's first name be that of her father's?

I didn't want to open that can of worms.

"Well, you see, son, there already was a Micah John – me. When you and I are together and someone says, 'Hey, Micah,' we know who they're talking to. And if someone says, 'Hey, Bobby,' or 'Hey, Robert,' we also know who they're talking to. Make sense?"

He nodded.

"I just wondered," he mumbled.

"Hey, Micah!"

My friend Morgan's voice called from the kitchen. I grinned at my son.

"So, who's Morgan talking to?"

Bobby grinned back and said in a loud voice, "You!"

Morgan's six-foot-four frame walked into the living room.

"Hey, there, Bobby!"

Still grinning, my son looked at me and said proudly, "Now Morgan's talking to me!"

"That's right."

Morgan looked from Bobby to me and back again.

"So what's this all about?"

I waved him off.

"I'll tell you later. How ya doin', friend?"

We shook hands and then Morgan sat in the recliner across from the couch.

"Well, I came to hear about the bear encounter. Could hardly believe it when I heard it."

"Dad got bit in the leg."

Morgan looked at my boy.

"He did? Did the bear lose any teeth biting into that rock?"

Bobby laughed and Morgan grinned.

"Ha, ha, funny man," I said.

Looking at Bobby I said, "Listen, son, would you go in the kitchen and see if any of Grandma's cookies are still left? I'm thinking your aunt Jill might have eaten them all, but if she didn't, would you bring some in here for Morgan and me?"

"Sure, Dad."

Bobby jumped up and ran into the kitchen.

"He's starting to ask questions," I murmured.

Morgan nodded and responded in a low voice, "I wondered. Asking about his first name?"

"Yeah. I dread the day he comes home from school asking about his mother."

"Heard from her?"

I shook my head and replied, "But with his fifth birthday coming up, I expect to."

"How are you going to handle it if she does contact you?"

"Haven't figured that out yet."

"You only have a few more weeks."

I nodded.

"So, what's this I hear about Hannah planning your parents' anniversary party?"

Before I could respond, Bobby skipped into the living room, a plate of chocolate chip cookies in his hand.

"Aunt Jill left us some!"

Morgan and I grinned at his happy announcement. Bobby moved the checkerboard and set the plate on the coffee table.

"Good boy. Thank you," I praised him.

"Your grandma makes the best chocolate chip cookies."

"Not anymore. Miss Hannah does."

Morgan and I shot a look at him and then at each other.

"What makes you say that?" I asked. "When have you eaten Miss Hannah's cookies?"

"Two days ago, while you were still in the hospital. She came by with some, said they were for all of us, and she asked me to save some for you for when you got home. Me and Grandpa ate most of them, so when we knew you were coming home from the hospital, Grandma made her cookies so you'd have some."

He covered his hand over his mouth and mumbled, "Oops! I don't think I was supposed to say anything."

Morgan laughed.

"They must've been really good cookies if you and your grandpa ate all of them."

Bobby frowned at him.

"Not all, most. Grandma and Aunt Jill each got one."

I could tell Morgan could hardly keep the laughter at bay.

"But none for your dad, uh?"

Bobby shook his head.

"I'm sorry, Dad," he whispered.

I ruffled his golden halo. He looked more like Ashley than me. I secretly hoped that would change as he grew.

"No problem. Doctor said I need to be careful how many cookies I eat," I told my boy.

"Should I put them back?"

"No!"

Morgan reached over and grabbed two goodies from the plate.

"What your dad can't eat, I can. My doctor said I'm fine to eat cookies."

I stared at my friend of fifteen years. Then I shook my head.

"Bobby, would you go find Grandma and see if she has enough supper if Morgan stays? I haven't seen him in a while and if she has enough food for all of us, I'd like him to stay. Would you go see what Grandma says?"

"Sure, Dad."

Bobby stood up again, and as he was about to take away the plate of cookies, Morgan snatched them from my son's grasp.

"I'll make sure your dad doesn't eat too many," Morgan said.

After a glance at me, Bobby ran out of the room and out the door. About to say something about the cookies, I was interrupted by my friend.

"So, about Miss Hannah ..."

Did I feel heat crawling up my neck?

Slightly changing the subject, I asked, "What are you doing Saturday morning?"

Morgan tilted his head and I answered his unspoken question.

"How would you like to make shrimp cocktails for my parents' party?"

"About as much as I'd ride one of those rodeo horses you tackle in the arena," Morgan responded.

I grinned slightly and then said, "You'll see 'Miss Hannah.' Maybe even Chloe."

This time Morgan's face turned slightly red. He bit into a cookie.

I chuckled.

Hannah

When I arrived at my aunt's house, where I've been living for the past eighteen months after leaving Seattle, I found her in the backyard caring for the colony of feral cats that lived in the two large wooden and wire condos she had constructed when I was sixteen. The deaths of my parents and uncle, her brother, sister-in-law and husband, in a freak private plane accident when I was fifteen, first brought me to live with Aunt Eileen. After meeting and dating Micah in high school, I had believed I'd live in the Highwood Hills area for the rest of my life, married to him and living at his family ranch.

But Micah, and God, it seems, had other plans.

After college and time in Seattle at an event-planning firm and then my aunt's broken hip nearly two years ago I returned to Highwood Hills, Montana. And I decided to stay.

The twenty-five cats in Aunt Eileen's care were spayed and neutered, thanks to her and a cat rescue organization in a community an hour away from Highwood Hills. They also worked together to help other towns and individuals care for cats either abandoned by people or born into a feral life. I admired my aunt's compassion for God's creatures, including humans at the local homeless shelter and women's safe house. Her support of local non-profits is one of the many reasons I love and respect my aunt. And of course, her care for me as an orphaned teen.

I watched her as she talked softly to the kitties, opened and poured out cans of cat food into different bowls. Some of the cats let her pet them, but most shied from human touch. Two of the previous strays shared our home as they came to the house last winter, likely abandoned because they were both friendly and craved human interaction. Now they, an elderly gray, short-haired male named Amos who was missing a canine tooth and an older, but not as old as Amos, female medium-haired calico named Tiger Lily, or Lily for short. They lived strictly indoors now and relished the warmth and affection we provided. And we relished their company, especially since my cousin, Emma, moved out a year ago.

I walked toward my aunt. Some of the cats scattered upon my approach. Aunt Eileen looked over and then straightened from her squatting position with a large smile.

"You're back. How'd it go?"

"Chloe's on track with the flower arrangements and Emma is finishing up the decorations, so all is good in those departments. I still need to check in on Patrick and Michael. I don't think the resort ballroom will be a problem – Michael's done thousands of these types of events – but Patrick, well, he's another case. He's still nervous about the shrimp cocktails and truthfully, not happy to have his kitchen invaded."

My aunt waved her hand.

"Leave Patrick to me. He'll be all right. How's Micah?"

"Recovering at home. He seems to be in good spirits."

"I still can't get over how the two of you were so unfortunate to run into a sow and her cubs this late in the season. Usually they're denning by now."

"It's the weather, Aunt Eileen. This long autumn we've had, with the warmer temperatures and sunny days. Their instinct to go into hibernation likely hasn't kicked in. We may have been unfortunate encountering her and the cubs, but we were fortunate nothing worse happened to Micah."

Aunt Eileen nodded.

"God was certainly with you both. Listen, I need to finish feeding these critters. I kept your lunch warm – it's in the oven on low."

I kissed her cheek and then said, "Thank you. I'll see you inside in a little bit."

She smiled and returned to her chores, and I turned and walked toward the house. Once inside, the two furry family members greeted me. Amos stretched his body along my leg, raising his paws. This was his signal to be picked up and held. I dropped my purse and brown leather business bag near the door and obliged the old cat. He wrapped his front legs around my neck, giving me what Aunt Eileen and I had christened 'The Amos Hug.' He rubbed his face on my cheek and chin, another way he showed affection, and his purring voiced his contentment. I smiled. Although at first these movements seemed invasive, both Aunt Eileen and I had come to understand and accept Amos's unique way of showing love and gratitude.

I returned his affection by rubbing my face on his cheek and whispering, "Thank you, Amos. You give such great hugs and love."

My phone buzzed, indicating I had a text. I set Amos back onto the floor and gave Tiger Lily a good chin scratching.

"Can't forget about our Lily girl," I cooed.

Not one for being held, Lily preferred lots of pets and scratches. Aunt Eileen and I had learned to respect the cat's space requirements and never forced her to do what she didn't want. Like people, cats have their individual personalities and preferences. Lily would sit on a person's lap if we were on the couch or one of the recliners, but she chose the who and when.

"I'll get you both something to eat. I guess I have food in the oven so I imagine you're hungry having to smell Eileen's good cooking."

The text buzzed again, reminding me I still hadn't looked at the message. After removing Aunt Eileen's chicken-cheese casserole from the oven, I checked the message. I didn't recognize the number, but in my line of work, that wasn't unusual. What was strange, however, was the area code: the message was from a Seattle phone number.

I hope I have the right number. I got it from H.R. Hey, Hannah, we miss you at the office. I miss you. I know things between us got heated, especially when you pressed charges for harassment and stalking. I'm sorry I scared you. Hope you'll come back to Seattle, come back to me. I'm a new man now. I guess it took a suspension and some required counseling to wake me up. Call me or send me a text back. Again, I hope I got the right number or I've just confessed stuff to a stranger.

I sucked in my breath and sat down hard on a kitchen chair.

I can't believe my former employer gave him my phone number!

Lawsuit for releasing private information jumped into my head. I bit my lip and looked at the ceiling. Then I hit the delete key, erasing my former colleague Jeremy Collins from my phone memory ... and hopefully from my life for good.

Micah

I stood on the deck that surrounded my parents' home as the sun set in the west. Tomorrow was the anniversary party ... and the shrimp-cocktail-making party. My sister, Jill, had agreed to help and I had arm-wrestled Morgan ... and won, so he was also on board. Hannah had told me earlier her aunt and cousin also planned to assist. When I questioned her about Chole, Hannah had responded, "She has a lot to do getting the floral arrangements to the resort and set up. Besides, I'm not sure she wants to be in the same room with Morgan. At least, not in a kitchen – too many dangerous objects for her to pick up and use on him."

"She'll be okay at the anniversary party, though, right?"

"The cutlery is just plastic, so, yeah, I think so."

I chuckled at the memory of the conversation.

Poor Morgan! We had both been dopes to drop good, kind, loving women when we were young. At least he hadn't followed my broken road and messed up even further.

But then I had Bobby. My marriage to Ashley had dissolved, but I had my son, and even though I no longer had a relationship with his mother, Bobby was a true joy and blessing. And not just to me.

The door opened and then closed. I glanced over and saw my dad step toward the porch railing.

"Another beautiful autumn evening," he commented.

"I can't get over how late in the year this weather has stayed around. I'm thankful to be here to enjoy it."

Dad looked at me.

"We're all thankful you're here, period. That bear encounter was a close call, Micah."

I shrugged.

"Could have been worse. I've been half-trampled by horses. No she-bear is going to keep me down."

"You're just lucky that 'she-bear' wasn't a grizzly – there's been more sightings of tracks and scats in the Highwoods this year. They're getting pushed out of western Montana with all the development and are setting up territory around here."

"Yeah, I've heard that from some of our neighbors."

"I personally look forward to the cold weather when they all go into hibernation."

A layer of silence enveloped us for several minutes.

"Mom and Jill and Hannah still in the kitchen?"

Dad nodded at my question.

"Gabbin' while they work, as usual," he replied. "Makes my heart happy to hear them."

I looked at him and grinned.

"Is that why you're out here instead of in there?"

My father chuckled.

"Oh, they've got stuff about tomorrow to talk about. They don't need me in the way."

Another moment of silence passed between us. That's one of the things I enjoy about my father – we can share each other's company without sharing a word, and we still connect. He could have disowned me any time during the past seven years, and he threatened to a few times, but I never doubted his love. When I brought Ashley and Bobby to the ranch four years ago and asked for his help in getting my life back on track, he welcomed me back with open arms. I certainly felt like the Prodigal Son Jesus talked about, and my dad, just like my Heavenly Father and the father in that story, embraced me and helped me turn my life around.

"I like knowing Hannah is back in your life."

My dad's statement caused me to look at him.

"You do?"

Dad nodded.

"Always loved that girl. Always knew she was the right one for you, and I'm glad you've finally realized it, too."

He looked at me.

"Don't get me wrong, I love my grandson, and I'm glad he's here with you, with us, but Ashley ... well, this kind of life wasn't right for her. And I never believed she really loved you. Nor you her. I know you've never really said anything, even after she left, and for Bobby's sake, that's good, but Micah, she wasn't the right woman for you."

I nodded.

"I know. I just wanted to try to make it work – for Bobby's sake."

"I know you did, and I respect you for that. But she chose to leave. She not only left you and this family, she left her little boy. And she never accepted Jesus as her Savior. The two of you were unequally yoked. That broke your mother's heart. Mine, too, really, especially knowing the kind of woman Hannah was ... is."

"I get it, Dad. I messed up when it came to Hannah, but I had Bobby to think about."

My father nodded again and replied, "Yes, and I'm proud of you for trying to make the marriage with his mother work out. I just want to say, if pursuing a relationship again with Hannah is something you want, and that God wills, well, your mother and I support it one hundred percent."

I studied his face. Although darkness prevailed around us, lights from the house cast their glow onto the deck. My father's blue eyes reflected sincerity and love.

"Thanks, Dad, I really appreciate knowing that."

He nodded. The door opened and closed once again, and my mother stepped outside. Hannah followed. Mom went over to my father, and he opened his arms. She enfolded herself into his embrace.

"What are you two men gabbing about out here?"

"Certainly not tablecloth colors and flower arrangements," Dad replied.

Mom chuckled.

"Well, I'd say not since the girls and I have all of that taken care of," she teased.

I looked from my parents to Hannah, and I found her eyes upon me. I followed my father's lead, opening my arms to the woman I love. In less than three strides, Hannah came to my side and enfolded her into my arms. Still a bit unsteady on my feet, I reached one hand and grasped the railing. Hannah helped steady me.

"I've got you," she whispered.

"Yes, you do, you most certainly do."

I looked over her head at my parents, who were watching us. Both of them smiled. I returned their expression and drew Hannah closer to my side.

Hannah

M y insides fluttered like a pavilion of butterflies as I stepped into Patrick's restaurant Saturday morning. My cousin and aunt would arrive later as I suspected Micah and his friend Morgan would as well.

"He thinks I'm crazy for trying this, but I reminded him we tried all kinds of crazy things when we were teenagers," Micah said last night. "I told him we just needed a mindset like we had eight, ten years ago," Micah had said.

"My thought is we make an assembly line," I responded. "Two people work on the cocktail sauce, perhaps my aunt and cousin, and three people work on the shrimp."

"Sounds like a good plan. Your ability to organize makes you a great event planner, Hannah. Thanks again for doing all this for my parents. Jill and I greatly appreciate it. We appreciate you."

I smiled. Hearing that affirmation, as well as the accolades from his parents, touched my heart. I knew God had given me a gift, and I was grateful to be able to bring joy to people during special occasions. But hearing words of affirmation helped confirm I was doing what I felt called to do ... and what I enjoyed doing.

I stepped farther into the restaurant, balancing a carrier of hot coffee with a tray of Aunt Eileen's apple-cinnamon bread. I knew the caterer would be in a stressed mood, I certainly was, but I continued to tamp down that emotion.

"Hey, Patrick! It's Hannah!"

"In the kitchen!"

I walked from the carpeted restaurant to the back of the building. As I reached the doorway, I heard male voices speaking in low tones. Slightly puzzled, I stepped into the large business kitchen. Three sets of eyes looked my way. Standing next to Micah stood Morgan, his best friend since middle school. The two had known each other three years before I moved in with Aunt Eileen. They had gone through 4-H together, played basketball on the junior varsity and varsity teams, spent time fishing and camping, and riding horses. Both were on the high school rodeo team. Whereas Micah pursued the sport professionally, Morgan stayed on his family's ranch. I had run into him just a few times upon my return to Highwood Hills, but because he remained in Micah's purview of friends, I had remained casual and aloof.

Now the two brawny men stood next to one another near a long, metal counter, and Patrick stood at the sink with a large silver-gray bowl in his hand.

"Hey, Hannah," Morgan said. "Nice to see you."

"Nice to see you, too," I replied. "Thanks for helping out this morning."

"Deveining shrimp? What else would I rather do? Um, let's see...."

"You're deshelling, not deveining," Patrick snapped.

"Good morning, Patrick," I said, adding an extra sweetness to my voice.

I held up the tray of sliced bread.

"Aunt Eileen and I made her famous apple-cinnamon bread."

I set the tray of warm, aromatic sweets on the end of the counter. I placed the four spiced chai lattes nearby.

"And picked up some chai from River's Edge Coffee Shop."

"You didn't think I'd have coffee going?"

Patrick's voice remained strained.

"Yes, but I thought you might want a break from that dark roasted stuff. Just bringing a touch of autumn to fire us all up."

"I'd say Patrick's pretty fired up all ready," Morgan commented.

"Watch it, kid!"

I looked at Micah and asked, "You doing okay?"

He nodded.

"Just thinking. Since the shells are on, that makes for an extra step."

"You see why I told her it can't be done?"

"Why didn't you just order unshelled shrimp?"

Don't push Patrick's buttons, Micah.

Before the restauranter could speak, I said, "Like Patrick said, Morgan can deshell, and you and I, Micah, can devein and put the shrimp in bowls. I have my aunt and cousin coming shortly and they will make the sauce."

"They can help me make the sauce," Patrick stated. "I have a special recipe and we'll be using it."

"That's great, Patrick," I responded. "I just didn't want to take you away from ...."

"Two of my workers are coming in to put the other appetizers together in a few hours. Then the rest of my catering crew will be here this afternoon. I've got the schedule worked out."

I gave him a dazzling smile.

"That's why you're the best – you're so organized!"

I glanced at Micah and winked at him. He smiled and winked back.

"So, for some energy to get going, how about some of Aunt Eileen's bread?"

I removed the plastic covering from the platter. Immediately, the fragrances of autumn in the form of apples and cinnamon arose. All three men caught the scent.

"Your aunt's bread always smells so good!" Morgan stated.

"Eileen is a terrific baker," Patrick agreed. "I wanted her to come and work with me, but she said baking for a thousand people a week was too daunting for her. I disagreed – said she could do anything she set her mind to – but she never took me up on the offer."

"She prefers baking for family and friends," I said. "It gives her joy."

I looked at Micah and asked, "How are your parents this morning?"

"Fine. Excited, especially Mom. You should see the flowers Dad had delivered already! A huge boutique of red roses, white lilies, and pink, red, and white carnations. It takes up nearly the entire island in the kitchen!"

I heard the joy in his voice, and I smiled. Micah loved to see his parents' affection for each other, one of the traits I adored about him. Just then a pesky thought tried to spoil my joy about his joy – how many large bouquets had Micah gotten for Ashley during their time together?

I physically shook my head to rid my mind of the question.

"What's wrong, Hannah?"

I gazed into Micah's eyes and, for a moment, sorrow tried to wiggle its way into my heart and the atmosphere. I pasted on a smile.

"Nothing. Just thinking how happy your mom must be."

Micah grinned.

"She is that."

"Well, if we're really going to make her happy, we need to get the shrimp ready for tonight," Patrick said.

"We have time for a piece of Eileen's bread," Morgan said as he reached for two slices. "Maybe even two."

"Hi, ho, everyone!"

Aunt Eileen's voice rang out from the restaurant.

"Back here, Eileen," said Patrick.

I chose a slice of the aromatic delight and asked, "I didn't see your truck, Micah."

"I hopped a ride with Morgan," he responded.

He showed me the ebony cane leaning against the metal counter.

"I still don't quite trust myself to drive. I'm going to give it a go on the ranch later and if I feel comfortable, I'll drive to the party tonight. Want me to pick you up?"

I shook my head.

"I'll be there many hours before you, or anyone else except Chloe. We have to put up the decorations and centerpieces."

"How is Chloe, by the way?"

Morgan's question caused me to look at him and respond, "Oh, she's fine. Her business is doing quite well."

"She seeing anyone?"

I studied the muscular rancher for a moment.

"Not as far as I know. I think her shop and her nature photography side-business keep her pretty busy."

"Umm, good to know."

Micah poked his friend in the ribs.

"Why'd you ever break up with her?"

"She dumped me, man, not the other way around. She said she didn't want to marry a rancher." He shrugged and added, "Her loss."

"Are you seeing anyone, Morgan?"

He looked at me with a slight grin.

"You asking me on a date, Hannah?"

I stared at him, dumbfounded, and then stammered, "Well, no, I just ... just was asking ... curious."

"No, Morgan's not seeing anyone, and I'm seeing you, so that's that," Micah quipped.

He stabbed the cane that he held upon the floor. I held up my hands as if being robbed at gunpoint.

"Whoa, easy there, cowboy. I'm just asking for a friend."

Morgan looked at Micah.

"Hey, man, I'm just goofin' off. I know she's your girl."

"Nobody's goofing off in my kitchen," Patrick snarled. "You young people – get your heads on straight and focus on the job at hand."

As my aunt and cousin entered the kitchen, Patrick changed his tune. He smiled and said, "Eileen! Emma! Come in, come in! Thank you for helping us this morning."

With a smile of her own, Aunt Eileen set a tray of muffins next to the bread plate.

"I didn't think the bread would last very long, so I made some blueberry muffins," she stated with a flourish.

I noticed her eyes twinkled when she looked at Patrick.

Umm. Could those two have something going on?

How fun it would be if my aunt and my favorite caterer fell in love and if Chloe and Morgan got back together! Especially now that Micah and I started re-establishing our relationship.

"Hi, ya, Emma," I heard Morgan say. "Good to see you."

"You, too," she responded.

"And Eileen," he drawled as his hand reached for a muffin. "No one beats your baking."

"I thought you liked my mom's chocolate chip cookies," Micah said, sounding a bit surprised and hurt.

"I do," his friend replied. "But Eileen outbakes every woman in this valley, including my mother."

"Gillian outbakes your mother," Micah said.

Laughter spilled forth. Morgan's mom did a lot of things well, but cooking and baking did not top the list.

"Speaking of your sister, where is she?" I asked Micah. "I thought you said she was coming, too."

"She is, but not for about thirty minutes. She's been doing extra chores since I got hurt."

"Okay, everybody, it's time to get to work!"

Patrick's announcement made us all scramble, except for Micah, who hobbled.

"Where do you want us, Patrick?" Aunt Eileen asked.

As Patrick gave out instructions, Micah hobbled my way. He pulled me aside and whispered, "Thanks again for doing all of this. You know my parents are very special to me, and if anyone planned their anniversary party, I'm glad it's you. To even make sure they have shrimp cocktail, bringing people together to help make that happen, well, I'm just grateful."

I smiled and squeezed his hand.

"It's my honor. Thanks for being here to help and for recruiting Morgan. We will get this done."

"Not if you don't listen and get to work!"

Patrick's scolding caused us both to laugh.

Micah leaned toward me and kissed my cheek. The tenderness was not lost on me. My heart melted.

"Save me a dance or two," he whispered. "I'll be the cowboy with the cane."

We chuckled.

His laugh ... oh, how I'd missed that delightful laugh! My heart whispered a 'thank you' to the Lord for bringing Micah and I together again.

Micah

That night, at the Highwood Hills Hot Springs Resort at the base of Highwood Mountain Range, I stood in the event room, near the food buffet. I leaned against a large wooden beam near the buffet table, an excellent spot for observing people as they filed into the room and watching my parents interact with their guests. I saw smiles on faces and heard joyful laughter. I couldn't help but smile as my parents engaged with friend after friend, neighbor after neighbor. I had always known my folks were well-liked and respected, but watching them now, in the midst of nearly one hundred area residents and another twenty or so relatives, I felt more in awe of them.

Dad's arm lingered around Mom's waist. His hearty laughter and the way his eyes twinkled when he looked at her made me admire him even more.

"Lord, help me to be more like him," I whispered.

I then caught sight of Hannah as she darted from one end of the room to the other. During the past hour, I had yet to talk to her. She was busy in her event-planner mode, ensuring the food and drinks were always filled, that the decorations were still in place, and that people were enjoying themselves. She caught my eye and gave a brief wave. I smiled at her and tipped my cowboy hat. She smiled back and then returned to her buzzing around like a honeybee zipping from flower to flower. Within moments, the band in the far corner struck up some instrumental music. As sound filtered through the room, I recalled something my grandfather said to me many years ago, when I dated Hannah my senior year of high school.

"Son, that's a fine young woman you've found. Don't let her go – she's good for you, and she fits well in our family. Look at how she puts up with me!"

I gazed at Hannah, now talking with her friend, the florist. The two women laughed, and, from my vantage point, I saw Hannah's eyes sparkle.

"Sorry I didn't listen, Grandad," I whispered. "I'm hoping for a second chance. If you have a little pull with our Creator, would you ask Him to help me?"

Her brown hair braided and pulled up onto her head exposed Hannah's suntanned neck and the Native American quill earrings that dangled from the lobes of her ears. The sky blue, three-quarter sleeved blouse and rainbow patterned, southwestern style skirt and brown boots she wore were simultaneously elegant and western, fitting the theme of the event ... and my parents' style. I glanced at my own attire – black jeans and suitcoat with a pale blue shirt and black bolo along with my best black boots. My parents had smiled their approval when I walked in and greeted them an hour ago. Dad wore similar clothing – Hanson men weren't much for tuxedos, although I had worn one on my wedding day. I glanced at my mother again. Rarely did she wear a dress, however, this special gathering took her on a shopping trip last week, and tonight, she simply glowed in the golden chiffon she wore. Gillian's outfit, a pale-yellow blouse and turquoise skirt with gold swirls, complimented Mom's attire. I thought the turquoise and silver boots were a bit much, but I'm not a twenty-two-year-old cowgirl.

"Hey, Dad."

Bobby's voice brought me out of my ponderings. I looked down at him. He looked dapper in his black jeans, dark blue shirt, and black and silver vest. Even his small, black cowboy boots remained shiny. In his hand, he held a plate of food.

"Yes, son?"

"Why is Miss Hannah ignoring us? She hasn't come over to even say hello. Did I do something wrong?"

I squatted down as far as I could. The leg injury still kept me from doing all I had been able to do previously. Lowering myself to Bobby's level was one of those remaining obstacles.

"No, Bobby, no one did anything wrong. Miss Hannah is in charge of Grandma and Grandpa's party, and she wants to make sure everything is just right. It's an important evening, for all of them."

"It's important to me, too. I want Grandma and Grandpa to be happy."

"Me, too, buddy, me, too."

I stood up, a bit off-balance but at least I didn't topple over.

"I think they seem happy, don't you?"

I glanced at my boy again, and he nodded.

"Yeah, they do. I'm going to take this plate of food to them and wish them happy anniversary."

I smiled.

"I think that would be a very good thing to do. With all these people, they might forget to eat."

Bobby walked away, balancing the plate of food between both hands. I watched him present the food plate to my parents. They each gave him a hug and then Dad took the plate from Bobby.

I decided to seek out Hannah and get that 'hello' Bobby, and I missed receiving from her. She stood near the gift table, straightening items and re-arranging table décor to make room for more items and cards given to her. The music's tempo increased and I saw my parents and a few other couples take to the dance floor. Hannah looked at me when I arrived and she smiled.

"Hey there, remember me? The cowboy with the cane?" I asked. "I think I asked you to save a dance for me."

Smiling, she responded, "I'm not sure how to dance with a cowboy who uses a cane. Are there certain special moves?"

"Any move you make is fine with me," I murmured.

Hannah leaned over and kissed my cheek.

"I'm sorry I've been so busy," she whispered.

"I understand. The party is great, Hannah. The looks on people's faces, including my parents, says it all. You've done an excellent job."

The smile on her face grew.

"Thank you. And the shrimp cocktails – they've gone over well. I guess you need to add 'shrimp cocktail maker' to your list of talents and skills."

I laughed.

"It was a team effort."

I extended my right hand and asked, "Ready for that dance?"

A shadow of concern passed over Hannah's face and she looked at my leg.

"Are you sure? Maybe we shouldn't take the chance."

"Now, I've been a good boy and gone to all of my therapy sessions, even a few extra so I could dance with you. Are you going to deny your man the opportunity to twirl you around the dance floor just because a bear bit me?"

Hannah smiled. Her beauty took my breath away, and I slipped my hand into hers. I began to lead her toward the dance floor.

"Well, hey, there, cowboy! There you are!"

I froze at the sound of the woman's shrill voice.

"Long time no see," she said.

I turned and saw a slight smile on my ex-wife's face.

"Did you really get mauled by a bear?" she asked.

"Ashley. What are you doing here?"

Hannah

It's really her!

My brain screamed as I stared at Micah's former wife. I dropped his hand from mine.

"I saw in the Great Falls newspaper where your parents are having this grand party – forty years, is it?"

"Since when do you read the Great Falls newspaper in France?" Micah asked.

Ashley gave a short laugh.

"I got back to the states six months ago. I've been doing a few projects, including a swimsuit edition, in California."

She turned to look at me, and, with a snarky tone to her voice, she said, "Be a dear, would you, and get me a glass of Chardonnay?"

"I'm not the wait staff," I replied.

"Oh. Fooled me, I guess. Well then, would you kindly ask someone to bring me a glass?"

Before I could reply, Ashley turned to Micah, and, draping an arm over his neck, she asked in a syrupy voice, "So, where is our son? He has a birthday coming up, and I wanted to surprise him. And you."

I felt my heart crumble. My eyes darted from Ashley to Micah. His face contorted. A moment ago, we had laughed and he had held my hand tenderly. Now I was an interloper. She was the mother of his child. They had a history. So did we, but their time together was more recent. I stepped away. As I turned my back, Micah stated firmly, "You're not part of this family."

I covered my mouth with my hand and felt tears sting the corners of my eyes. Though I wanted to run and hide, I held my head high and walked stalwartly away from them.

I increased speed as the back room came into view. However, when Nadine Hanson stepped in front of me, I came to a stop. I avoided her gaze at first, trying to compose myself.

"Oh, Hannah! This is so wonderful! John and I are enjoying ourselves ... What's wrong, dear? You're pale."

I forced a smile and attempted to look at her.

"I'm just ... Sometimes organizing and putting on the event catches up with me. I just need a few minutes ...."

"Oh, yes! You've been going a mile a minute all night, all week, in fact. Micah told us you're also putting together Bobby's birthday party. He shouldn't have asked that of you, especially with this event and Thanksgiving coming up."

"Oh, I've got that handled. In fact, changes are in the works – Micah's not going to need my help with Bobby's ..."

I nearly choked as tears threatened.

"With the birthday party."

Nadine studied my face.

"Hannah, something's wrong. What are you not telling me?"

I didn't want her to see me cry, so I excused myself before I lost control. As I briskly walked away, I heard John say, "Nadine, do you see who Micah is with?"

I glanced back. The Hansons were staring toward the doorway, and I looked in that direction. Micah and Ashley strolled out of the room and through the door.

"Great party, Hannah! You've done it again!"

My cousin Emma's words broke the dam. I choked on a sob and ran to the back room, praying no one was in there. I leaned against a table and let the tears flow. I bit my lip to keep the sobs from spilling out. I didn't want anyone to know where I was or what was happening, so though I cried, I kept my voice muffled. Blood from my lip dripped on my tongue, and salty tears ran down my cheeks. I bent over a table, feeling as if someone had punched me in the stomach. A few seconds later, kind, comforting hands squeezed my shoulders. I glanced up.

Emma looked at me with concern in her dark brown eyes.

"What is it, Hannah? What happened?"

"Ash ... Ashley. She's come back and ... and Micah is ... he's with her."

Emma's face turned almost white.

"Can't be," she whispered. "She's been out of his life for, what, three years or so?"

I laughed slightly.

"Well, she's back now and they have a son together."

"Maybe it's a misunderstanding."

"He said I wasn't part of the family."

Emma stared at me.

"He said that?"

I nodded.

"I'm not Bobby's mother, that's for sure."

"I'm going out there and give him a piece of my mind."

I caught Emma's arm.

"They left," I whispered. "Together."

Tears streamed down my face. Emma enfolded me into an embrace.

"Oh, Hannah! I'm so sorry."

I cried on her shoulder. I heard the door open and shut, and I stepped back, wiping my eyes.

"What's going on in here? Why aren't you two ...?"

Chloe's voice stopped for a moment. I kept my back to her.

"Hannah? Emma? What's going on?"

"Seems that cad of a Micah Hanson has broken her heart again."

"What?!"

"Ashley is back."

"Is that who I saw him leave with?"

A sob ripped through my throat. I covered my mouth with my hand.

"Chloe!"

Emma's reprimand caused me to lift a hand.

"It's okay," I whispered. "I know what I saw, too."

"I don't understand," Chloe said.

"Micah. Ashley. Together again. What's not to understand?"

The harshness in my cousin's tone made it unmistakable how she felt.

"Together?" Chloe asked. "As in romantically?"

"Are you really that dense?"

"Emma. It's not her fault," I said.

"I am not dense, and I don't think they're together, at least in that sense," Chloe huffed. "Micah had a hardened look about him, and I heard them arguing with each other on their way out the door. I think she's here to make trouble."

I looked at Chloe, and then Emma and I looked at one another.

"Well, I know what I heard," I told them. "Micah reminded me I'm not part of the family. She's Bobby's mother. She's family."

"But they're divorced," Chloe said. "She's not part of the family."

"I'm sure he wants her to be," I responded. "She's Bobby's mother and she's beautiful. She's a model. I can't compete with that."

Emma's hands enclosed over my forearms.

"You don't have to compete. You are you, and if that's not good enough for Mr. Famous Bronc Rider, so be it. There's a man out there who will appreciate you for who you are, a lovely woman inside and out."

"I thought Micah was done with all the pretense, that he was back in church and that things were going well between the two of you," Chloe said.

I shrugged.

"I thought so, too, I really did."

I straightened my shoulders and wiped the tears from my eyes and off my cheeks.

"Well, I'm not going to let this break me. He's made his choice. I have a celebration to see through to the end. Emma, would you please ask your mother to help ensure everything's going all right for the next fifteen minutes? And Chloe, would you please help me with my make-up? We have two hours to go – I need you both to help me get through the rest of this evening. I'm going to fake it to make it, and then I'm done with the Hanson family ... forever."

Micah

After I dropped Ashley off at her hotel in town, refusing her advances and offerings, I drove to the edge of the river outside of town. After parking the pick-up, I ambled outside, strolling – and limping – along the water's edge. Anger coursed through my veins and I felt like screaming. I grabbed a pebble from the sandy soil and threw it, like a skipping stone, but with vigor.

"Argh!"

Between tossing the rock and letting out a verbal frustration, I clenched my teeth and kicked a nearby log.

"Ow!"

I shook my foot.

"Great, Hanson! What if you broke a toe?"

Aggravated with myself for letting Ashley get under my skin, I snapped a dead branch from a nearby cottonwood tree. I gazed heavenward and asked another question aloud.

"Lord, why now? Why bring her back into my life now?"

I took a deep breath and started limping along the riverbank, the cane helping to steady my steps.

"Thank you for keeping Bobby from seeing her and thank you for keeping her away from my parents," I said aloud. "Thank you that I have the money to get Ashley out of our lives for good. Even though I have to start over and rebuild the reserves I had on hand, I'd rather do that than have my son's heart broken by her comings and goings. Please protect his heart. You know I'd rather give her the money than lose Hannah either."

I took a deep breath to steady my emotions.

"I don't understand the 'why' but Your Word says that your ways are greater than our ways and that humans are prone to evil. Ashley never really loved me, did she, Lord? All she ever really wanted was my family's money. Thank you for opening my eyes to the kind of person she is, the kind of person I was, and thank you for bringing me back to You and to my family. And thank you for bringing Hannah back into my life."

I took one more deep breath and then I cast my eyes onto the waterway. The full moon reflected upon the river, causing light rays to dance across the meadow beyond and streams of light to tickle the ripples on the water. I watched the small waves trickle across rocks. I looked farther downstream, and I envisioned the anger, disappointment, and frustration inside of me travelling with the water, cascading over small boulders, and out of sight.

A new type of serenity enveloped me. I focused on the blessings in my life: my son, my family, my friends, Hannah, God's grace, His creation, this beautiful night.

"Cast your cares upon Him, for He cares for you."

That scripture ricocheted through my heart, soul, and mind. I stared at the moon and whispered, "Lord, I give my cares to you. Thank you for caring for me."

AN HOUR LATER, I RETURNED to the resort. Only the cleaning crew remained. My heart fell, realizing I'd missed most of my parents' celebration. I stepped into the hallway near the room's entrance and stepped into an alcove, cell phone in hand. My fingers found my call list and I scrolled for my dad's number and punched the OK button. After three rings, he answered.

"Micah. Where have you been, son? We were about to come looking for you."

"Ashley showed up at the party. I needed to get her out of there before anyone, especially Bobby, saw her."

"He's been asking for you since you left."

"I'm sorry. I had to deal with his mother...."

"And just how did you do that?"

I noticed the undertone of anger in my dad's voice.

"I'm sorry I left the party, Dad ...."

"You left with her. A lot of people saw you, including your mother and me."

"I am sorry, Dad, really. I just wanted her out of there."

"Hannah saw you, too. And a lot of our guests. There's talk ...."

"I'll deal with all that later. I'm paying Ashley to stay away from us, from this town, and from Bobby. We're meeting tomorrow at the courthouse, and I'm having papers drawn up, legal papers, having her relinquish all parental rights and requiring her to stay away from us, from all of us."

"And she's agreed? What prevents her from doing what she did tonight – from just showing up?"

"Money. Lots of money."

I took a deep breath and then said, "Dad, I'm giving her my trust fund."

My father didn't speak for a few moments. I waited.

"Son, that's a lot of money. What your grandfather left you, what your mother and I put away for you, what you've set aside from your winnings...."

"I know, Dad, but it's the only way to keep Ashley from disrupting our lives again. There's more money to be earned in the coming years. I'm only twenty-six. I never told Ashley about the horses I intend bringing on next year – she thinks it will always be cattle, and I never told her anything differently. She wanted half of the oil royalties, too ...."

"Why, that conniving ...."

"Dad, it's under control. I told her that belongs to you and mom and that you and I have agreed those funds go to Bobby for his education and inheritance. She tried to argue that, being she was the one who gave birth to him, she would legally have a right to the money because I would inherit it before Bobby. I told her that was not the arrangement, and I reminded her she received the funds I had made rodeoing during the two years we were together, and that it wasn't my problem if she spent it all already. I also reminded her she had a career and was making money, and since I'm leaving the rodeo circuit after this last event on New Year's Day, she'd be making more money than me."

"Son, are you sure this is what you want to do? You don't owe that woman any more than you've already given her."

"If the trust fund keeps her out of our lives, it's worth it – for Bobby's sake."

"Okay, well, then so be it. Where are you?"

"At the resort. I didn't realize how long I'd been gone. I needed to get my head together after that fiasco of her showing up. How's Hannah? She seemed a bit upset when Ashley waltzed in."

Again, my father stayed silent for a few moments.

"Dad?"

"She is upset, Micah. She wasn't the happy, smiling girl she had been earlier. She told your mother and I she was fine, but her eyes were red and puffy and she didn't say much the rest of the night. Your mother asked her to come for dinner tomorrow night and that we'd give her the rest of her payment, but she asked us to mail the check to her. She used 'tired' as an excuse, and I'm sure she is, but her demeanor and the lack of sparkle in her eyes told us something else."

"I'll call her and talk with her."

"Maybe wait until tomorrow. Why don't you come home and spend time with Bobby? He's worried."

"Yeah, okay. So sorry I missed most of your party, Dad. And I'm sorry Ashley just walked right in. I told her she was no longer family and that she had not been invited..."

"You said that to Ashley?"

"Yeah. I know it wasn't Christian of me ...."

"That's not it, son. Hannah's cousin, Emma, told your mother and me that Hannah heard those words, and, Micah, she thought you said them to her."

"What?!"

"She heard you, Micah, and she thought those words were meant for her."

"Dad, that's not true, that's not it at all!"

My heart sank. I put my hand on my head. How in the world could she think such a thing?

"Dad, I gotta go. I need to talk with Hannah immediately."

Before he could respond, I hung up. I punched in Hannah's number and I heard the ring. Another ring. Then another. After four rings, her voicemail picked up, and after the message, I said, "Hannah, it's me. I'm sorry about tonight at the party. I think we have a misunderstanding. Please call me as soon as you get this."

I hung up and then sent her a text, thinking she might see that before listening to her voicemail.

Instead of typing, I dictated the words.

So sorry for skipping out of the party. I had something I needed to do, something important to take care of. I need to talk with you about what happened tonight. Call me ASAP.

I placed the phone in the back pocket of my jeans and then left the building, ambling out of the large establishment and through the parking lot with my cane. After unlocking the truck door, I climbed into the driver's side seat, and closed the door, I laid my head on the steering wheel.

"Lord, help Hannah to see my text soon and call me. Help her to understand I love her, not Ashley. Help us both clear up this situation. I don't want to lose her again."

Hannah

For the millionth time, I read Micah's text and listened to his voicemail. Dawn hadn't yet come – neither had sleep. My mind kept seeing Ashley's slender arm encircling Micah's shoulder and neck, the red, strapless mini-dress hugging her body and amazing curves, and her wavy, blonde hair cascading across her shoulders. A model. A famous bronc rider. No wonder the world adored the couple and mourned when they split up. Well, the world will rejoice once again at their reunion.

I squeezed my eyes trying to get the image to go away. Instead, I envisioned newspapers, magazines, and online publications flashing photos of the couple, both with large smiles, and little Bobby grinning from atop his dad's shoulders. A cry escaped my lips. I jumped out of bed and went to the window. After parting the curtains, I stared at the darkness. What I saw outside my window reflected what was inside my heart – blackness, a dirty, sootiness that choked and strangled, much like smoke that engulfs a community during a fire.

"How could he do this to me? Just when I began trusting him."

My spoken words sounded like the whine of a child. I didn't like that. I was not going to let Micah win this time. I wasn't eighteen anymore. I had lived in a big city, gone to college, and worked at a large event-planning firm. I had made a good living, and, except for one other broken relationship and a stalking incident, I focused on a career without a man in my life. That other relationship had not been as hurtful as with Micah the first time, but still, afterward, I told myself, "No more dating." And after my co-worker stalking and harassing me and my aunt in need of care, I took those as signs to leave Seattle and start over again in Montana.

Now, here I stood, at my bedroom window feeling bruised and broken once again. My resolve returned – No. More. Dating. It was time I moved on. I thought I'd healed from seven years ago. Helping my aunt and establishing myself as an entrepreneur, reconnecting with some friends and making new ones here in Highwood Hills had shown me I could do the small business and community involvement well. If I could do it here, as well as in Seattle, I could certainly do it again. Somewhere else.

My phone chirped. A text message. And early in the morning. Surely not...?

I picked up the cell phone. Yes, it was him. Again. Well, of course, he's a rancher. I put the phone down without checking the message.

Check other things instead.

I walked to my desk and turned on the small lamp then I turned on my computer. I could set up my own business in a different town, maybe even a different state. Staying in Montana, though, made better sense – I could still visit my aunt, cousin, and friends on weekends, certainly longer, holiday weekends. And I've had area clients who could provide references.

I sat down on my office chair, drawing the bathrobe around me tighter. Overnight, the temperature had dropped. My heart felt cold as well. I didn't pray, didn't seek God's direction, I just went into research mode. Although I felt a nudge from the Holy Spirit, I ignored the prompting. I was not only angry at and hurt from Micah, but I also felt like God had let me down, that he had opened my heart to loving Micah again and then let my heart break like a piece of Emma's pottery.

No more, the shards screamed.

Saving money the past few years added to my inheritance and so starting over in a hopping place like Missoula or Bozeman would be easier financially than when I left Seattle. A new year approached.

New year, new goals, new me.

Telling my family and friends, however, would be difficult. I decided to wait until I did more research. Where might there be room in those larger, growing communities for an event planner? Should I buy a place or rent? I knew housing was at a premium in those locations but I also had some connections. I began making a list of people I knew in different areas of the state and after that list was completed, I brought the internet up on my computer and started looking at real estate. At first, I became downhearted as I reviewed prices of homes for sale and places to rent. Then, something caught my eye.

FORECLOSURE. 3-BED, 2-BATH, ALONG YELLOWSTONE RIVER. FIXER-UPPER. BEING SOLD AS-IS. 2-ACRE LOT. $157,000. INQUIRE AT BIG SKY BANK, COLLIER, MT.

I could have a hobby farm with some animals and I could easily work out of the home while also still providing a bedroom and bathroom for guests, like my aunt or cousin or friends. There wouldn't be much business in Collier, population barely four-thousand, but larger towns like Billings and Bozeman were within driving distance – both places could serve as client possibilities yet I'd live away from those communities and have a tranquil place of my own. Maybe I could even start an animal rescue, helping my aunt with what she tries to do.

That would keep me occupied and not thinking about ... No, I'm NOT going there!

I flipped through the photos offered about the property. My heart sank. Each room needed a great deal of work. The house had been heavily lived in – and not kept up. Marks on the painted walls indicated children had been given free-rein to use crayons to make "masterpieces," and flooring was old and faded. I bit my lip. Maybe this idea was going to be more difficult to work out than I thought.

My phone rang. I glanced at the clock – six-thirty. Must be Micah. Only ranchers called people before daylight.

"I don't need you, or want you, Micah John Hanson," I said aloud. "I have a life, and you no longer have a part in it."

I stood up, opened the bedroom door, and walked downstairs. My aunt's gray tabby cat greeted me when I arrived in the kitchen. I bent down to stroke Amos' soft fur.

"Good morning, Amos. I hope you slept better than I did."

After petting the cat a bit longer, I rose and walked to the counter where the coffeepot waited. Aunt Eileen always ensured we had fresh-brewed coffee each morning by filling the basket and machine the night before and setting the timer for six-thirty the next morning.

While the liquid brewed, I gave Amos a small helping of canned food and refilled his dry food bowl. I also rinsed out the water dish and refilled it. The noises of moving around the kitchen brought Tiger Lily running. Despite my misery, I smiled. These animals brought joy with their simplicity and acceptance. I filled another food dish and set it in front of Lily, and I said, "Here you go, little miss. No, I won't leave you out."

I watched the two cats consume the food before them. The thought dawned on me that they had gone through misery in their lives, and yet, they trusted people to take care of them. They didn't harbor bitterness toward all humans for the abuse bestowed upon them by one or two. They allowed grace, and the kindness of others, to guide them.

"Lord, help me. I just don't know if I can be like you or these cats."

My grace is sufficient.

The Scripture rang through my heart and my brain. I recalled the writing of St. Paul when he was experiencing a severe trial. Could God's grace be sufficient for me now, during this time of trial and heartache?

Micah

I walked out of the courtroom, feeling free, but knowing I was nearly broke. Understanding my financial situation was a lot worse than it was yesterday, or even two hours ago, I wondered if Hannah would even be interested in pursuing a relationship anymore. I also recognized my trust of women was now also lacking. Maybe they were all like Ashley – greedy and selfish.

I shook my head as I walked to my truck. That thought's from the devil, I told myself. My mother, my sister, my female friends – they weren't that way. People around here, in and around my community, weren't like that. Everyone worked hard and one rancher who wasn't as well off as another was still treated kindly and with respect. No one in my circle of friends was arrogant or flamboyant – we were all neighbors and we cared about one another. Look who had shown up for mom and dad's anniversary celebration. More than one hundred people, from all walks of life. My parents never looked down on others or thought themselves better than, even after oil was discovered at the back area of the ranch before Grandad died.

For the millionth time, I asked God to forgive my younger self.

As far as the east is from the west, so far have I removed your transgressions from you..

That verse from Psalm 103 spoke loudly to my heart, mind, and soul, and I again thanked the Lord for His mercy.

I sat in the pick-up, and I called Hannah's number. Again, no answer. I decided I'd just go to her Aunt's house after finishing what needed to be done at the bank. Now that Ashley's name was printed and signed on the document and the paperwork legally filed, I needed to get all this business with Ashley finished and out of my heart and mind. Afterward, I had business to finish with Hannah, and a new journey to walk.

I turned on the truck motor and pulled out of the parking space, away from the courthouse. I drove the five blocks to the bank that the Hanson family used. My heart felt slightly heavy at the loss of the funds that I wanted to save for my eventual retirement, marriage that I hoped would happen in the future, and for my son. But I had sought God's direction and guidance, and I knew I had made the right decision.

I'm young enough to start over, I reminded myself as the truck drew closer to the bank. *Bobby will be fine, we will be fine. God, Your will be done. I trust you, and I again thank you that Ashley will be out of our lives for good and that I can start over again. I look forward to building up the horse aspect of the ranch and see where You lead me on this path. Thank you, God, for second chances.*

I parked the truck in the bank's parking lot and walked inside.

AN HOUR LATER, MY TRUST fund was signed over to my ex-wife, and I opened a new account with a lot less money in my name and my father's name, with Bobby as beneficiary. I walked out of the bank with less weight on my shoulders than I'd experienced in several years.

It was now time to start over.

I drove to Chloe's Floral Shop, where she read me the riot act. I explained the misunderstanding and asked for the largest bouquet of white and yellow roses with white lilies and cedar sprigs she could create. I hoped the large smile on Chloe's face would hyperspace to Hannah's.

After leaving the flower shop, I drove to Eileen's house. I purposefully left the cane in the truck, and I hobbled up the two steps to the porch. I rang the doorbell and tried to steady my rapidly beating heart. The door opened, and Eileen stood in front of me.

"Micah!"

Her voice noted her surprise. I doffed my brown cowboy hat.

"Hello, Eileen. I've come to see Hannah."

"I gathered." She nodded at the big bouquet of flowers in my hand. "Very pretty. Unfortunately, Hannah isn't here."

"Look, I don't know what she's said to you, but I believe she has a misunderstanding about the other night."

Eileen closed the front door and placed her hands on her hips.

"Oh?"

"She told you she saw me with Ashley."

"The entire gathering saw you with Ashley. I have to admit, I thought more of you and your parents ...."

"None of us knew she was coming. She wasn't invited."

Another surprised look crossed Eileen's face. Her stance took a less offensive position.

"Oh. I, uh, we, none of us knew that."

"Well, my parents did. And truthfully, Hannah should have known – she had the guest list."

"I think she was in too much shock to think about a guest list."

"So, Eileen, will you please let me see her? We need to clear up this misunderstanding."

"Honestly, Micah, she isn't here. In fact, she left town."

I felt an arrow hit my heart.

"What? Left town? What do you mean?"

"She said she has a lead on a possible event planning job in Billings, so she's on her way there. She said she probably wouldn't be back until the day before Thanksgiving."

"Oh. A job, in Billings. Like a job-job or an I'm-planning-the-event-job?"

Eileen smiled slightly.

"The second one."

"So, she's not moving?"

Eileen frowned and then responded, "Well, I don't think so. She didn't say anything about that."

I handed the cellophane-wrapped flowers to her, saying, "You might as well enjoy these while she's away."

Eileen resisted.

"Oh, no. Give them to your mother. Afterall, it's your parents' anniversary week."

"The house is loaded with flowers, from dad, me, my sister, and from the party. Our house looks like Chloe's Floral Shop on steroids."

With a smile, Eileen accepted the offering.

"Well, in that case, all right."

"Ah, Eileen – when you learn Hannah's returning, would you let me know? I really do need to talk to her."

She nodded and said, "Yes, I'll give you a call. I imagine it will be Wednesday. She and I have pies to bake for the homeless shelter for Thanksgiving."

"That's a very nice thing for you to do."

I placed my hat on my head and then tipped it again.

"Have a good day."

"You, too, Micah. Thank you again for the flowers."

I gave her a quick smile and said, "My pleasure."

As I walked down the steps down to the sidewalk, I heard the front door close. I removed my cell phone from the back pocket of my jeans, and, after unlocking the truck, I called my father. Climbing into the vehicle, I heard him answer, and I said, "Dad, will you meet me in town for lunch? I have some things I'd like to talk with you about."

"How'd it go with Ashley?"

"Okay. Everything's done, and she's on her way out of town and out of our lives."

"What else is going on, son?"

I sighed and stared down the street.

"I'm wondering about me and Hannah. Maybe we're not meant to be after all. She's left town, Dad, and I'm not sure she's coming back."

Hannah

After looking at the house in Collier and spending some time in Billings, I drove out of the city with a sense of disappointment. The house needed more work than I believed I could handle, emotionally and financially, or even wanted to deal with. Cracked walls from an unstable foundation. Totally new paint needed in the entire house. Floors that required replacement. Fractured windows. A musty, not-lived-in-for-a-while smell.

A person would likely be better off demolishing the entire house and building a new one. That, however, wasn't what I wanted. At least, not right now. Although the area had its own loveliness, and charm I wasn't sure I wanted to put permanent roots down here, at least not in the form of buying land and building a new house.

Clouds gathered the farther east I drove, adding to my gloominess. Perhaps after the holidays my spirits would lift. I realized in the two days I was gone from Highwood Hills, the idea of not spending Thanksgiving and Christmas with Micah and his family had a major effect on my mood as well as seeing him with Ashley's arm around his neck. At least, I had made an in-road with a potential client in Billings – the friend of a friend whose daughter was graduating college next spring. I was thankful it wasn't a wedding – I wasn't sure I'd be able to handle that type of event yet.

I pulled off for a quick lunch break an hour out of Billings. From the drive-through lane of the Burgers'N'More, I called my aunt. After she answered, I said, "I just wanted you to know I'm on my way back.

I'm getting some lunch right now, but I expect to get in about three hours from now."

"How did things go in Billings?"

"Not as great as I'd hoped, but I think I have a spring graduation event. I'll know for sure in January."

"Well, at least it's something. Maybe that one will turn into two or three."

"Maybe. I think I'm going to just wait until after the holidays to pursue any other possibilities. Everyone's focused on Thanksgiving and Christmas."

"Well, don't forget you have Bobby's birthday party in early December."

"Umm, that's not going to happen. Micah tried to call me again, so I sent him a text to stop and said that I would no longer be planning Bobby's birthday party. He and Ashley can do it. Afterall, Bobby is their son."

"Hannah, I think you should know ..."

"Gotta go – it's my turn to order. See you in a few hours."

I hung up and made my lunch order, and then I drove out of the lane and back onto the highway leading to Highwood Hills.

THREE HOURS LATER, I pulled into the driveway of my aunt's house. I sighed. Somehow, I was going to have to get through the next few months. For now, I had pastries to help bake. Every year, Aunt Eileen baked four pies for the homeless shelter and delivered them. Last year, we stayed and helped serve the meal because my cousin Emma spent the holiday with her boyfriend, Todd, and his family.

This year, she and Todd planned to come to Aunt Eileen's, and originally I had planned to eat with them first and then go to the JBarN for a later-in-the-day meal. Micah had invited me two weeks ago. But with Ashley's return, that all changed.

I shuddered as I thought of her in the house, laughing with Nadine and Jill and helping them in the kitchen, while Bobby played games with his father and grandfather. Before my thoughts traveled farther, I got out of the car. I pushed the button to open the trunk, walked back, and grabbed the suitcase. I closed the lid and strolled towards the house.

I stopped on the small porch. Instrumental music played inside the house. *Beethoven*, I thought.

I smiled slightly. Just like Aunt Eileen – playing music while preparing the Thanksgiving meal. Or baking pies. Both, likely, knowing her. She always liked to get a head-start on holiday meals.

I tapped on the door briefly and then unlocked it and walked inside.

"Aunt Eileen, I'm back!"

I rounded the corner from the foyer and set my suitcase near the stairway. No response from my aunt. I turned and saw the back of her head near the top of the couch. *Funny, not my aunt's hair color.*

Then the person stood and faced me. I caught my breath.

"Welcome back."

That amazing baritone voice. I nearly collapsed.

"Micah," I whispered. "What are you doing here?"

"We have some things to talk about."

Micah

I watched Hannah grab the stairway banister as she seemed about to faint. Forgetting my injury, I rushed to her. I put my hands around her waist as she nearly collapsed.

"Come sit down," I murmured, my angst turning to concern.

I led her to the couch, and she sank into it.

"Sorry," she whispered. "I just got back from a short trip ...."

"To Billings." I nodded and then continued, "Your aunt told me. Did you get some new clients?"

"I may have, yes. I'll find out after the holidays."

I kneeled beside her, moving the coffee table out the way. I winced as pain shot up from the wounds.

Thank you, bear.

However, I determined to look into her face so I silently prayed for strength. My leg relaxed and the pain alleviated. I looked into her green eyes.

"Hannah, are you ... are you leaving Highwood Hills?"

I could barely get the words out. She avoided my gaze.

"I ... I don't know," she whispered.

I took her hands in mine and continued looking at her.

"I don't want you to go."

Hannah bit her lip and looked at the ceiling and then out the living room window.

"Please look at me, Hannah."

She didn't.

"Hannah, please. There are some things I want to tell you, but I need you to look at me so you can see my eyes."

Instead, she stood up and pulled her hands from mine.

"I can't do this, Micah. With Ashley back in your life ..."

"She's not."

That made her look at me. I stood with some difficulty. Realization dawned on her face and she exclaimed, "Your leg!"

I waved her off.

"I'm mending."

My eyes locked onto hers, and I said, "There's more important things to talk about right now."

I took a deep breath and then exhaled and said, "You didn't answer my calls or texts so I came ..."

"Why should I? We don't have anything to talk about."

"That's where you're wrong, Hannah. Like I told you, Ashley isn't in my life."

I walked to her but kept my hands to myself.

"I need you to understand some things, and the biggest thing is, I didn't ask Ashley to come to the party."

"The point is she did come and she's the mother of your child."

"That's all she is."

"And that's a lot."

Hannah crossed her arms across her chest and whispered, "I can't play these games, Micah."

"There are no games. At least not from me. I did not ask Ashley to be at the party, and we are not together."

I stated each word firmly, hoping she understood and accepted the truth I spoke. Hannah stood her ground. Her arms remained crossed. and she looked me in the eyes again.

"Sure looked differently to me with her arm draped around you."

I heard the hurt in her voice. My heart ached to fix the pain.

"Ashley is a vixen. She plays games. I don't."

I held my hand out to her. With a smile, she accepted the gesture and placed her hand into mine. As we slowly waltzed, I looked into her eyes and whispered, "I still have a way to go to be the man I want to be, but I think I'm on the right path. Especially with you at my side."

Our eyes met again for a brief moment, and then Hannah laid her head on my shoulder. I closed my eyes as I held her in the dance, and my heart whispered another 'thank you' to God.

Hannah

The next morning, I nearly danced down the stairway. I smelled baking pies and knew Aunt Eileen had already started on the tasty treats to take to the homeless shelter and the women's shelter. I shook my head. My aunt never ceased to amaze me.

I waltzed into the kitchen and called out, "Good morning, Aunt Eileen! Happy Thanksgiving!"

She looked at me from her position at the stove and smiled.

"The same to you, dear. All is well, I take it."

I kissed her cheek and popped a few blueberries into my mouth.

"Yes. Things could not be better."

"No running away?"

I gazed at her and my jolly mood sank.

"Running away?"

My aunt smiled and responded, "I found the listing you printed out when I emptied the trash this morning. What were you thinking, Hannah? That place needs to be demolished!"

She smiled, and I smiled back.

"Tell me about it!"

"Next time, if there is a next time, talk to me about it first."

"I don't expect there to be a 'next time,' Aunt Eileen."

"Neither do I, my dear, neither do I."

She returned to stirring a pie filling cooking on the stove and added, "Cinnamon rolls are cooling near the sink, and the egg casserole is being kept warm in the second oven. Micah will be here soon – he's offered to help deliver the pies. So has Patrick. I invited them both to join us for our Noon meal. I suspect you'll go with Micah to the ranch for his mother's evening meal?"

I nodded and answered, "That's what we talked about last night. I guess I should grab a quick shower if Micah and Patrick are coming by soon."

Then, her words really hit me and I turned to look at her.

"Patrick? Aunt Eileen, are the two of you …?"

She smiled, and I noticed a blush rise to her face.

"I've been a widow for more than a decade, and I've known Patrick for twenty years. I think I'm ready to take a chance again. He wants to court me, and I said 'yes.'"

I chuckled and then I kissed her cheek and said, "Funny, those are the words Micah said to me last night. I'm happy for you, Aunt Eileen."

I walked from the kitchen toward the living room and on to the stairway. As I placed my foot on the first step, the front doorbell rang.

"I'll get it!" I called out to my aunt.

I grabbed a sweater from the nearby coat rack and wrapped it around my southwestern-patterned lounger suit. When I opened the door, a large bouquet of fall flowers greeted my eyes and nose. The aroma of sunflowers, carnations, and roses and the beauty of the arrangement adorned with baby's breath and willow sprigs caused me to smile.

"Oh, Micah! They are gorgeous! My goodness, why did you …?

A face from the past peered around the large glass vase. He frowned and then growled, "And just who is 'Micah?'"

I took a step backward and stared.

"Jeremy," I said in a hoarse whisper. "What are you …? How did you …?"

He gave me his sly grin.

"Surprise, my dear. I figured if you weren't coming to me, I'd come to you. And on such a festive, wonderful occasion!"

He stepped toward the open door. I began to close it. Jeremy blocked my attempt.

"Now, now, is that any way to treat a man who has brought you this lovely gift and taken his holiday to track you down?"

"You need to leave – NOW!"

My aunt's voice called from nearby.

"Hannah, let him in!"

"You heard the lady," Jeremy sneered.

He pushed the door open, causing me to nearly fall. He grabbed my waist but I wrenched my body from his grasp.

"Don't touch me," I hissed.

"Dear, who is it?"

My aunt's question, and her approach, caused Jeremy to reach over and lock the front door. He turned to look at my aunt and gave her a flourishing smile as she stared at him from the edge of the kitchen.

"Ma'am," he drawled. "My name is Jeremy Collins, and I used to work with Hannah. I'm sorry to pop in on this wonderful holiday, but I wanted to see her again since it's been so long."

He presented the vase of flowers to her.

"I hope these will make amends for my intrusion."

Aunt Eileen looked from Jeremy to me. I gave a slight shake of my head. She returned her gaze to Jeremy.

"Well, um, Mr. Collins. You've traveled quite a way. I have coffee and some cinnamon rolls in the kitchen, if you'd like to come in."

No, Aunt Eileen, no!

She walked to Jeremy and gave him a smile.

"Thank you so much for the beautiful boutique of flowers. They are exquisite!"

My aunt led Jeremy to the kitchen and as she did so, she turned her head slightly and nodded toward the stairway. I took the hint and, as my aunt occupied Jeremy, I glided up the carpeted stairs and to my room. I locked the door and picked up my cell phone. I pressed 9-1-1 and when the operator answered, I said, "Please! Send some officers to my aunt's house. We have an intruder!"

I gave the operator the address for the house and I stayed on the line as she instructed. And I prayed. I prayed even harder when I heard Jeremy yell, "Where's Hannah? What did you do, old woman?!"

A crash sounded in the kitchen. I whimpered and then whispered into my phone, "Hurry, please!"

Micah

I had to park the Gladiator on the street. Hannah's 4-Runner and another SUV, one with Washington state license plates stood idle in the driveway. I frowned, not recognizing the silver Lexus. I didn't recall either Eileen or Hannah mentioning anyone from Washington planning to visit. Although I knew Patrick was to be at the house and I didn't know what type of vehicle he drove, he'd surely have Montana-issued plates because he had opened the restaurant in Highwood Hills more than twenty years ago.

I remained puzzled as I walked up the drive toward the house. Hearing a crash radiating from inside and a man yelling, I quickened my pace. The pain in my leg increased, but I chose to ignore it. I felt the need to get into the house quickly. Upon reaching the door, I jiggled the handle – locked. I pounded my fist on the large, wooden barrier.

"Hannah! Eileen! It's Micah. Let me in!"

Eileen shouted my name, and then I heard another crash and a woman scream. I also heard Lily and Amos squeal and hiss.

I pounded on the door again.

"Let me in!"

Hannah's soft voice said my name. I looked around. No sign of her. Then her voice called my name again. I peered around the brick column and looked up. From her second-story bedroom window, Hannah waved at me.

My heart leaped. Whatever was going on, she appeared to be safe. That left Eileen. I looked toward the door again.

"Micah, he's in the kitchen," Hannah's hoarse voice trickled from the second floor.

"Who? Who is it, Hannah?"

"The guy from my company."

The stalker! How did he get here?

I looked at the driveway. That's HIS Lexus.

"I've called the police," Hannah said.

"Is there another way into the house? I need to get your aunt."

A pounding echoed from Hannah's room. She turned her head from me.

"He's here!"

"I don't want to hurt the old woman, but I will if you don't come out, Hannah!"

I forced my two legs to move quickly until I was under her window. I glanced around. The ledge under the window would hold her and the waterspout might, but then, it might not. I prepared myself to catch her.

"Hannah, look at me."

She complied.

"Climb out the window and on to the brick ledge. Then close the window and climb down to me."

"What? No way. I can't do that."

"You can and you must. I'm here. I'll catch you."

She looked skeptical. Until she heard the stalker's voice again.

"One last warning, Hannah. I came in good faith, brought you flowers, just wanting to see you. Why are you shutting me out?"

With one more look at me, she opened the window wider and climbed through. After settling her feet on the brick ledge, she reached up and closed the shutter. I watched as Hannah inched her way along the edge. Sirens from police cars startled both of us and she nearly fell. She saved herself by grabbing the spouting along the side of the house. I stood underneath her, prepared to catch her.

"You're doing good, Hannah," I encouraged her. "I'm here, I'm right here."

The sirens drew closer. I kept my eye on Hannah. I heard her bedroom window open. I forced myself to concentrate on Hannah as she maintained her hold on the pipe.

"Hannah! What are you doing? Come back here!"

The stalker's voice caused her to look toward him. Her grip loosened, and, with a scream, Hannah tumbled toward the ground. I prepared myself, locking my knees and holding out my arms. I had to take a few steps to the right. I caught Hannah in my arms. The force of her fall landed us both on the ground, but I continued to hold her.

Tires squealed and voices came to me but I held onto Hannah.

"Are you all right, Micah?"

Her whispered question and our awkward situation caused me to laugh.

"Yeah, yeah, I'm good. How about you?"

"Scared."

"Miss, sir! What's going on here?"

I looked up from my sprawled position on the ground. Before I could respond, Hannah said, "A man broke into our house. My aunt is inside, and so is he."

The police officer helped Hannah up and another uniformed officer assisted me. We all turned at the sound of a car engine.

"That's him!"

Hannah pointed to a man who had leaped into the driver's seat of the Lexus. The guy looked at us, fear showing on his face. He jammed the SUV in reverse and began to steer the vehicle down the drive. The two officers gave chase. I began to follow, however, another cruiser pulled in just below, and the intruder's Lexus slammed into the side the police car. Four officers converged and I saw the stalker raise his hands as all four aimed guns at him. I watched the man be dragged out of the damaged vehicle, searched, and then handcuffed.

Hannah's arm encircled my waist. I looked at her.

"I never dreamed this would happen, not here, anyway," she whispered.

"You're safe."

I placed a hand on her cheek and re-stated, "You're safe."

Hannah's eyes widened.

"Aunt Eileen!"

Hannah ran toward the house. I followed, each pounding step feeling like a bone breaking in my leg. We reached the porch and found the front door open. Eileen stood in the doorway, hand on her head and watching the officers with their prisoner.

"My goodness, what a morning this has been!" she stated.

"Oh, Aunt Eileen! Are you all right?"

Hannah's worried voice came to my ears.

"A pounding headache, and my kitchen is a mess, but otherwise, yes, I'm all right."

At that moment, one of the officers said, "Sir, sir! You can't be here. There's been an incident ...."

"The love of my life lives here. I need to be sure she's okay."

We all watched Patrick run towards us.

"Did I hear what I think I just heard?" Hannah whispered.

I smiled.

"I think I know where the pie-baking will commence today," I whispered back.

Hannah

And we did. We finished the pies at Patrick's restaurant and took them to the two shelters. Later, since my aunt's house was a crime scene and we had to give statements and stay away the rest of the day, Patrick and my aunt cooked the Thanksgiving meal. Micah and I and my cousin helped with side dishes and then, while the turkey baked, we all went to the local waterfall and took a leisurely walk, relishing the crisp autumn air. The temperature had cooled from the previous week, but we still basked in the fall colors and the mild weather. A few hours later, we savored the Thanksgiving meal.

Later that night, I relished another family meal, this time with Micah's parents, sister and her boyfriend, and Bobby. I found their presence heartwarming.

During the next several weeks, Micah and I spent a lot of time together. In my heart, I apologized to God for my many doubts, and I felt peace wash me afresh.

On Sundays at church, my aunt and I sat in the same pew with Micah and his parents and sister. Morgan and Chloe also attended services with us. I noticed their happiness and that made me happy. In fact, joy totally filled my heart.

The Advent season took on an extra-special meaning. Micah's rich baritone voice touched my heart as we sang holiday hymns. We read Scripture and prayed together each night on the phone. Dinners out and meals in, whether at Aunt Eileen's or at the ranch were filled with deep discussions, card and board games, laughter, friends, and family. And on those occasions when we dined alone, we shared about our previous lives, the good and the bad. We listened to one another and comforted each other. No judgement. The past was the past. I knew I had crossed over from grudges to forgiveness, and I thanked God for His help in doing so. I even forgave myself for the trail I'd traveled, being reminded by Micah and my aunt that God had forgiven me, so I needed to forgive myself.

My thoughts of moving away vanished. During my personal prayer time in the mornings, I gave my fears and concerns to God. I asked Him to direct my days and take away my worries. He answered by slowly alleviating the desire to move, which really would have been running away. My relationships with my family and my friends, with my business, and with Micah and his family strengthened. So did my faith.

Micah's parents warmly welcomed me when I visited the ranch. Their sincere smiles and loving hugs told me they approved of me dating their son again. One early December day, while waiting for Micah to saddle a pair of horses for an outing, his sister, Jill, put an arm around my shoulder as I stood at the picture window looking at the beautiful sunny day.

"You and Micah are a great couple," she said. "I believed that then and I still believe it. I'm glad you're back together."

"Took a bit of time for that to happen," I responded.

"Yeah, but you're both better for what you've been through. Bobby is one of the best things that happened to Micah even though the boy's mother is a selfish, spoiled ... well, we won't go there. Micah's matured, he's no longer a prodigal by family or by faith, and he's got a great lady in you. We all love you, you know, Hannah."

I looked at Jill and smiled.

"I'm coming to realize that."

She squeezed my shoulders in a sisterly hug.

"Are you going to continue barrel racing next year?"

Jill nodded and dropped her arm from my shoulders.

"I think I still have a few good years, and with Micah settling in at the ranch and Bobby to start school next fall, I won't be doing as much babysitting. Hopefully, I'll get into more competitions and place higher on the circuit."

"I imagine you'll miss spending as much time with your nephew."

She nodded again and then said, "I will. But this is a year of change. Bobby turning five and living at the ranch fulltime, Micah giving up the saddle bronc riding for life at the ranch, dad cutting back more, and having you back in our lives ... well, it's going to be an exciting and different year for all of us."

I looked at Jill.

"Do you really think ... do you think it might be too much too soon?"

She returned my gaze and replied, "It's a lot, but no. Micah needs this. He needs stability. He needs you. Am I wrong to think you never stopped loving him?"

I didn't answer for a moment, just looked at her. Then I shook my head. I gazed out the window again and saw Micah walk out of the barn leading two horses: a sorrel gelding with a white blaze and a red appaloosa mare.

"How did you know?" I whispered to Jill.

"The day we came back from the road, when we arrived two days early, I saw your expression. And then during mom and dad's anniversary party. Your eyes – every time you looked at my brother, your eyes held a longing, a sadness like, but your smile reflected love. I saw in you what I've seen in Micah for the past seven years – even though he tried to hide it with his party face and his stubborn, selfish attitude. Eyes don't lie – they reflect the heart and soul."

No one had ever said anything like that to me. Had I truly carried a torch for Micah others saw in my eyes all these years?

I felt Jill's arm around my shoulders once again. I looked at her, and she returned my gaze.

"The two of you are going to be okay this time. I really believe that," she whispered. "Trust your heart, Hannah. Trust Micah. Most of all, trust God. He brought you back together. You each had lessons to learn before the timing was right. He knew, so just trust Him."

My head nodded slowly. Micah walked into the kitchen and peered around into the living room where Jill and I stood.

"Horses are ready. Are you?"

I looked from Jill to Micah and then back again.

"Yes. Yes, I am most certainly ready," I said.

Micah

Two days after the horseback ride with Hannah, I stood in the barn once again, this time in a stall next to a palomino pony. I placed a blue woven saddle blanket on the little horse.

"You and my son are going to be good friends," I told the pony as I readied the saddle. "You're his first horse, and that makes you extra-special. My first horse still lives here at the ranch. He's a bit bigger than you, but then I was raised with horses. Bobby's been around them, but not on them so much. With your help, that's going to change."

"Bobby's going to love him."

I glanced over toward the barn door, and a smile dawned on my face as Hannah stood there, sun cascading through the window and across her hair and face. She took my breath away.

God, you've truly sent an angel, I thought.

I've sent the woman you love, to love you and your son.

With a glance upward, I silently gave thanks.

Aloud, I said, "You really think he'll like this pony? It is somewhat small."

Hannah took a few steps toward the stall, saying, "It's a pony, Micah. It's supposed to be small. My first horse wasn't much bigger when I first started riding, if you remember. And I was going on sixteen."

I grinned at the memory.

"It was a Welsh pony, and yes, she was bigger than this guy," I responded.

Hannah, now standing at the stall, stated, "Not much and I was taller than Bobby is. That makes a difference, too."

I leaned against a post.

"How can this be, Hannah? How can my son be five years old? He was just learning to walk not long ago. Or so it seems."

"I'm sure our family members would say that time flies, especially when raising children. You're a dad and you and Bobby are hitting milestones. This is one of them."

I looked at her. Our eyes connected. I again gave thanks to God from my heart that He allowed me this second chance.

"I'm glad you're here," I whispered.

"I'm glad I'm here, too," she replied softly.

I reached out my hand and cupped her cheek. My thumb rubbed her chin, and she leaned into the embrace. I wanted to say more, but I held back. Today was Bobby's day – our time would come. I smiled at her and, dropping my hand from her face, I then turned and reached for the saddle.

"Everyone's up at the patio," I told Hannah. "I plan to be up there in a few minutes."

"Aunt Eileen is already up there," Hannah responded. "I came by to let you know we were here."

After saddling the pony and securing the bit and reins, I turned back to Hannah with a smile.

"I'm sure Bobby's going to love the glove and ball you picked out for him. You know I told you that you didn't have to get him a gift."

She smiled.

"Who attends a birthday party and doesn't bring a gift?"

Her eyes twinkled. I smiled back.

"Well, I know he'll love it."

"I was able to add another element to his gift."

"Oh? How so?"

"You'll see. I think you're going to like it, too."

"Now you've got me very curious!"

"Good!"

Continuing to smile, Hannah opened the stall gate.

"So, what's the pony's name again?" she asked.

"Cedar. At times, when the light hits his coat just right, a hint of red ripples through the golden color, reminding me of the bark on some of the cedar around here."

Hannah rubbed the little horse's nose.

"Cedar's a fine name for this guy," she said.

I walked out of the stall holding the pony's bridle. He followed me without a command.

"Want to walk with us to see the birthday boy?"

"Of course," Hannah responded. "Aunt Eileen took Bobby's gift to the house already."

I smiled.

"I think Bobby's going to have a fine day."

Hannah smiled back.

"I think so, too."

We walked side-by-side, hand-in-hand, toward the house, Cedar following. As we walked alongside the large, log home, laughter came from the back area. The atrium my father constructed five years ago for my mother created a glassed-in area for entertaining during most of the year. On extra-warm days, Mom put up blinds to keep sun and heat from overwhelming her plants and any person who wanted to spend time in the room. The orchids, peace lilies, ferns, and jade plants offered color and tranquility and provided respite after long days in the field or as snow piled up at the ranch during winter.

Although the day was partly sunny, the 40-degree temperature reminded us that winter wasn't long to arrive, and therefore, the atrium served as the birthday gathering. I could see Bobby hopping around as the adults lounged on comfortable couches and chairs spread throughout the room.

"I think your sister's hop-scotch game has Bobby occupied," Hannah said in a low voice.

I nodded.

"That was his first gift of the day, given to him at breakfast. My parents' Lego set came next. We told him the other presents would come this afternoon."

"What about the gift from his mother?"

"A set of trucks. Those will arrive tonight before bedtime. Along with a book I'm giving him – his own Bible."

Hannah smiled.

"That's wonderful, Micah. I was thinking about getting him a book of Bible stories and a book about the birth of Jesus for Christmas. Would that be okay?"

I took her hand and squeezed it.

"Perfect!"

As we approached closer to the atrium, Bobby looked out and saw us. His eyes lit up, and when he saw the pony, I heard him squeal. He rushed to the front of the glass and pressed his face against the windows. I motioned for him to come outside. My mother, my sweet, always-prepared mother, slipped a coat on my son, and Bobby dashed out of sight for a moment. I heard the side door of the house open and bang shut.

"Door, son!"

"Sorry, dad!"

And then he ran toward me and Hannah, his eyes glowing and fixed on the pony.

"Is it mine? Really for me?"

"Yeah, son, it is."

Bobby's small arms encircled my waist and then quickly he turned and hugged the pony's neck.

"What's his name?"

"Cedar. When the sun hits his coat ...."

"I love him!"

I chuckled and glanced at Hannah. Her large smile as she watched Bobby hug the pony again endeared her to me even more.

"You'll be able to go with your dad more often now, Bobby," she said.

"Like you do, Miss Hannah?"

"Yes. You can go riding with us, too, on your own pony."

"I'd like that ... a lot."

"So would I, son," I said. "Want help up or can you climb into the saddle yourself?"

"I want to try it myself," Bobby said.

He placed his boot in the stirrup and slipped into the saddle with ease.

"You've been practicing," I acknowledged.

He grinned.

"Yep. Aunt Jill's been helping me with one of the smaller horses. The older one that hangs out with your old horse."

I smiled.

"Ah, Dusty."

"That's the one."

I glanced at Hannah and found her staring at me.

"Dusty?"

I nodded, smile still on my face.

"You still have her."

Hannah's remark wasn't a question, but an awed statement.

"She's a great little horse. Jill learned to ride on her, just like you did. She makes a great pasture companion for Storm in his old age. We also have some burros I adopted the last few years."

"I can't believe your family kept her. I never wanted to ask what happened ..."

Hannah leaned over, her body slightly touching mine.

"Thank you," she whispered. "Will you take me to see her sometime?"

"Of course. I also want you to meet the burros and donkeys we have. I'm thinking about putting together a little petting zoo for kids, and I'd like your help in planning some events around that."

Hannah stared at me.

"When did all this come about?"

"Oh, I've had the idea for the past year. I talked it over with my parents about six months ago, and they liked the concept. Bobby does, too, don't you?"

My son nodded his head vigorously.

"I love animals!"

I tousled his hair.

"I know you do. We all do."

I glanced at Hannah and my eyes twinkled at her. She smiled.

"Yes, we all love God's creatures and His creation."

"How about the three of us take a short walk later and you and Dusty get reacquainted?" I suggested.

"I'd like that," Hannah murmured.

"Hey, Dad! Can I ride Cedar now?"

"We'll do a short walk around the house. You still have gifts to open. Then, in a bit, we'll go for a ride, you, me, and Miss Hannah."

"Cool!"

I laughed, and as Hannah and I walked side-by-side, I led Cedar with my son atop his first horse. I leaned toward Hannah and whispered, "So, how is this courting thing going, in your opinion?"

I grinned and she chuckled. She slipped her hand under my elbow and said softly, "I think your grandad and great-grandad would be very pleased with your courting ways. I know I am."

Our lips met in a soft, delicious kiss.

"Hey!"

Bobby's admonishment caused us to break the kiss. I looked at my boy.

"You gotta wait to do that."

"Wait? Why, son?"

"Married people do that. You two aren't married yet!"

I looked at Hannah. I could tell she was trying not to laugh.

"Good point, Bobby, good point," I said.

A LITTLE WHILE LATER, I learned what Hannah referred to while we were in the barn. Her gift to Bobby was not just a baseball glove and ball, but also tickets to spring training in Arizona for the following February. As I stood near her that night on the porch, after the horseback ride and family dinner, I whispered, "Not just Bobby's birthday present, but an early Valentine's gift for us. February in Arizona – great idea!"

She smiled.

"Well, the tickets are actually for you, Bobby, and your father. I thought it would be a great way for the three of you, three generations of Hansons, to spend time together."

At first I was taken aback, but then, no, it was a sweet gesture. And I was stepping a bit out of line. Something else had to come before a trip together.

"I will be in the area, however."

Hannah's statement caused me to look at her once again. And she smiled again.

"I have an event in Phoenix, a conference I'm helping organize, thanks to a friend in Seattle."

"Conference? What conference?"

"A conference for event planners. How ironic is that?"

We both laughed.

"Well, you'll be good at that," I said as our chuckling died down.

I touched her cheek tenderly and then I whispered, "Thanks for what you did for Bobby and for my family. I'm glad you're back in my life, Hannah."

I placed my other hand on the other side of her face, and then I dipped my head and placed my lips upon hers, kissing her firmly yet tenderly.

I hoped Bobby wasn't watching.

Hannah

Winter arrived two days after Bobby's birthday. Snow lay on the ground and clung to now-leafless oak and aspen trees as well as the evergreens. The dazzling snowflakes that fell from the sky added to the essence of Advent.

Christmas trees graced both families' homes, a medium-sized one at Aunt Eileen's and an eight-footer at the Hanson house. Helping decorate both trees, Micah and I shared memories of Christmases past, times we were together and times we were not. We listened to each other's stories as we hung ornaments, garland, and lights sipping on cider my aunt simmered on the stove while she and my cousin and Emma's boyfriend also shared memories of their Christmas times.

While at the ranch, I became more acquainted with Micah's family and their Christmas memories, re-stoking the times shared with them when I was younger. Images of Micah's grandfather came to mind as we each told a story about him, helping Bobby to learn more about his great-grandfather that he'd never know. Hot chocolate was the drink of choice for the tree-decorating time at the Hanson household. By the time that large evergreen was covered in silver tinsel, red and white balls, glowing lights of various colors, and western ornaments such as horses, saddles, sheep, trees, and trucks, as well as a nativity scene, a star, and topped with an angel, the grandeur of the fir reflected the majesty of landscape.

"So beautiful!" breathed Micah's mother.

"It's the best tree ever!" Bobby announced.

"You did a great job helping, buddy," Micah said, picking up his son and giving him a hug.

I smiled. Being part of this family again during this special time of year brought a song to my heart. Aloud, I started the Christmas hymn, "Oh, come all ye faithful, joyful and triumphant..."

Each Hanson family member joined in, and when I heard little Bobby sing, still in his daddy's arms, I reached over and touched his hand. The boy looked at me, grinned, and enclosed his fingers around my hand. Micah then clasped both of our hands into one of his, and we stood there, the three of us, close to one another physically and emotionally, as we all finished the song.

This seemed like the perfect culmination of the past ten days spent with Micah and his family. Dinner dates, horseback rides, walks in the snow either in moonlit nights or snowy evenings – each moment shared brought Micah and me closer in mind, heart, and spirit. We held hands. We danced. We engaged in snowman-building and snowball fights with Bobby. The little boy's hugs around my waist brought joy to my heart and tears to my eyes. I not only fell back in love with Micah, but I also fell in love with his son.

Little niggles of doubt still plagued me. If Micah and I didn't make it, this time not only would my heart break because of us, but it would also rip to shreds because of Bobby. And what about the little boy? He no longer had his birth mother in his life – what would happen to his young heart if I also wasn't part of his life?

Late afternoon on Christmas Eve, I decided to share my concerns with Aunt Eileen. As we wrapped gifts for the Hansons to send home with them tonight after church, I said, "I'm wondering what Bobby will think if his dad and I don't make it?"

I fingered the book of Bible stories I had purchased for the boy as one of his Christmas gifts.

"How can Micah and I claim to be Christians and possibly break that little boy's heart?"

"What kind of talk is this?"

I looked at Aunt Eileen. She was staring at me with her hands on her hips.

"Where is this coming from? You're not going to break that boy's heart because you and Micah aren't going to break up."

"We didn't make it seven years ago. What makes you think we'll make it now? And what does that even mean? He and I haven't spoken once about the future – he's just said we'll take it slow."

"He went through one divorce with the boy's mother. I'm sure he wants to go slow so you and Bobby have time together and Bobby accepts you. And you accept him."

I chuckled and then said, "Oh, I've accepted him all right."

"You love the boy."

Oh, Auntie, you are preceptive!

Instead of speaking, I chuckled again and said, "Oh, for sure. And if Micah and I don't make it, my heart will not only break, it will shatter. I love both of them, and I don't think I'll survive if this relationship doesn't."

My aunt walked over and placed her hands on my arms. Keeping her eyes fixed on mine, she said in a tender voice, "You and Micah have many people praying for you and your relationship. We all know you love each other, and we all know the fears you each have. But, God knows, too, and I highly doubt He'd have brought the two of you together again if His blessing wasn't on your relationship. Just trust Him, Hannah. I've told you that before. God wants what's best for you. And for Micah. And for Bobby. You and Micah are walking with the Lord in a deeper way now than either of you were seven and eight years ago. Believe He brought you together for good, not for heartbreak, and especially not to break Bobby's heart. Our loving Lord doesn't work that way."

I studied her face a moment and then gave her a hug.

"You're so wise, Aunt Eileen. I just wish these doubts wouldn't keep cropping up."

She smiled.

"Christmas is all about love and miracles. Think about how Mary must have felt, all the doubts that ran through her mind, after Gabriel announced she was chosen to bear the Christ child. Think about the time, the setting, the status of women back then, especially to be pregnant and not married. But God had a plan, a much bigger plan than any human could understand. Mary kept her eyes on the Lord and followed where He led. She believed. She had faith. Was it tested? I'm sure because again, look at when and where she lived. Try to emulate Mary, the mother of our Lord – believe and follow. Have faith that God wants to work for your good. For Micah's good. For Bobby's good."

I smiled and nodded.

"Now, let's finish wrapping these gifts so we can be ready for church!" Aunt Eileen commanded.

"Yes, ma'am!"

FOUR HOURS LATER, MY aunt and I sat in a pew of the festively-decorated church, singing the final hymn of the evening. Patrick sat on the other side of Aunt Eileen. Their courting was well-known and accepted in the community. The same could be said of me and Micah. The Hanson family and my cousin and her boyfriend took up seats in the same pew and the one behind. Also joining in the Christmas Eve service nearby were Chloe and Morgan. As per our usual during the past few weeks, Micah and I sat next to each other. Often during the service, our fingers entwined, and tonight was no different.

Love and joy filled the sanctuary – and my heart and soul.

A mid-sized blue spruce stood in the corner of the altar area, adorned with white bells and red balls and a large strand of colorful lights. White candles on the altar added to the light in the darkened sanctuary as we all sang *Silent Night* while additional candles flickered in the windowsills. Voices low but blended together in reverence as we sang the beloved hymn. White garland decorated the railings to the altar and red bows attached to the hallway-side of the brown, wooden pews.

Smiles and twinkling eyes appeared on the faces of those around me, and I felt a joy so deep, tears glistened in my eyes.

For the tenth time that night, I whispered a grateful prayer in my heart not only for reuniting me with Micah and his family, but also for the meaning and purpose of Christmas – to send Jesus into the world to save humans from their sins and one day reunite all who believe in heaven with Him and our Heavenly Father.

I felt a nudge to my ribs. I glanced up at Micah, and he gave me a questioning look. I smiled to reassure him I was all right. His arm slipped around my waist, and he gave me a quick hug.

At the completion of the song, the pastor stepped down from the altar and stood in front of the congregation.

"I want to wish all of you a very blessed and merry Christmas. I know many of us like to stay and visit, but I ask that we do so in the foyer or outside. I've had a special request from one of our congregants, and I want to honor that request. So, please, everyone, make your way to the foyer where you'll find cookies and other refreshments if you'd like to enjoy those while visiting with friends and family."

The organist started to play *What Child is This*, and people began to file out from their pews, many whispering.

"I wonder what that's all about?" Nadine Hanson commented as she and John began to leave the pew. Micah and I followed them, and then he caught my hand, stopping me beside him.

"Ah, Mom, Dad, would you take Bobby out with you? Jill, Eileen, Emma, would you mind going with my folks for just a few moments? There's something I need to speak to Hannah about."

I looked at him.

"What's going on?"

Micah gave me a brief smile.

"Just be patient."

Then he looked at his parents again.

"Mom, Dad, please?"

I noticed John tried to hide a smile, and when I looked at Nadine, her smile was wide. Quickly, though, she turned to her grandson, who stood beside her.

"Come on, Bobby, let's see what kind of cookies the good ladies of the church made."

"Hooray, cookies!"

John and the others followed them, but not after Aunt Eileen gave my hand a squeeze. As they filed down the walkway toward the foyer, I looked at Micah.

"Micah, what...?"

I couldn't finish my question. Still holding my hand, he led me closer to the altar. Then, taking both of my hands into his, he dropped to his right knee. My eyes widened.

"Micah!"

"See, I'm making progress. That Mama Bear can't keep me down!"

I smiled and actually choked on a laugh.

"Now what is all this ...?"

He interrupted.

"Hannah Anne Donovan, there's something I want to ask you."

My eyes widened again, and I removed my right hand from his and placed it on my mouth. With a large smile, Micah reached into the pocket of his dark blue suit jacket.

"Hannah Anne Donovan, would you do me the honor ...?"

"Oh, yes!" I exclaimed, not letting him finish.

His smile deepened.

"Can I ask the question first?"

"Oh, sorry."

"Hannah, before God, I profess my undying love for you. You stole my heart when we were still in high school and it still belongs to you. And so, since you have my heart forever, would you do me the honor of being my wife forever?"

"Yes, yes, oh yes!"

From the black velveteen box, Micah withdrew a half-carat diamond surrounded by smaller diamonds and rubies. I stared at the glorious gift. He slipped the ring onto my fourth left finger. Although a bit small, I considered the snugness another source of commitment – that ring wouldn't be coming off easily!

We both chuckled.

"I guess this is true commitment," I said, wiggling the ring on my finger.

"It's certainly the start. The other one comes later and I'll make sure it's snug, too."

"Micah, this is way too grand. If I'm going to be a rancher's wife, we don't have to spend ...."

Micah rose.

"This is what I chose for you and it's what I want you to wear. Without worry."

I bit my lip and then started to open my mouth to mention Ashley. A Voice spoke into my heart.

Trust Me. Trust him.

Tears formed in my eyes. Micah reached his right hand and gently wiped the moisture that began to travel down my cheeks.

"Everything's fine, Hannah," he whispered.

I smiled and nodded my head.

"Not just fine, perfect," I said softly.

He wrapped his arms around me and my arms encircled his neck. Our lips met in a tender, sweet kiss, then Micah deepened the kiss, taking my breath away. Our lips waltzed and then two-stepped, and he pulled my body closer to him. Neither of us heard the doors between the sanctuary and foyer open, but we did hear the pastor clear his throat. I stepped away from Micah and smoothed my red and black dress.

"I take it the outcome of the proposal was good?"

"Ah, yes, pastor, thank you," Micah said.

I heard embarrassment in his voice.

"Good, because there are about fifty people waiting out here who want to hear the news."

Micah looked at me and grinned. I smiled briefly, also embarrassed, but he reached out his hand and I enfolded mine into his. We walked down the aisle toward the pastor. Micah whispered, "Makes for good practice."

I laughed, a hearty, joy-filled laugh, and when I looked forward, I saw a large smiled on the pastor's face. He extended his hand.

"So, a Valentine's Day wedding?" he asked.

I shook his hand, and smiling, I looked at Micah.

"Well, I assume so since we have tickets to spring training in Arizona," I said.

"That's what I hoped you'd say," Micah said, a twinkle in his eye.

He shook the pastor's hand and asked, "So, are you busy on Valentine's Day?"

"I am now."

The pastor looked from Micah to me and back again, and then he said, "Merry Christmas and Happy New Year to you both!"

"And to you as well, pastor," Micah responded. "We'll be seeing you soon."

Micah extended his arm to me, and I slipped my hand under his elbow.

"Ready to face them all?" he asked.

I nodded and then I glanced at the ring again.

"It's very beautiful, Micah."

"As are you, Hannah," he whispered. "Merry Christmas, my love."

"It is, it certainly is!"

His lips met mine in another tender, yet passionate, kiss.

As the pastor opened the doors to the foyer, I interlocked my fingers with Micah's. Thundering applause greeted us. I smiled at the crowd and then looked at Micah. His face beamed. Bobby ran up to him, and Micah picked him up. The boy kissed his father's cheek, and then he looked at me.

"Are you going to be my mom who doesn't travel and stays at the ranch most of the time instead?"

"Would that be okay?"

"My dad asked the same question two days ago. I told him I'd like that a lot. Is it okay with you if I like that idea a lot?"

I smiled.

"It's definitely okay because I like the idea a lot, too."

He leaned toward me, arms open wide. I glanced at Micah, whose eyes glistened with tears. He nodded. I opened my arms, and Bobby fell into them. He hugged my neck, and I returned the little boy's embrace.

"Well, family," Aunt Eileen began, a choke in her voice, and her hands clasped into Patrick's, "I believe we have food and music waiting at my house, and a lot to celebrate."

"And tomorrow, it's Christmas dinner at our house," said Nadine.

I looked at my big, beautiful family and my heart expanded. God's blessings were all around me – this wonderful group of people, the amazing landscape where we all lived, the church, my friends, this community, and the amazing gift of Christmas – God's love in human form. Love surrounded me, and I felt deep, abiding gratitude.

Micah kissed my cheek and whispered, "Are you happy?"

Before I could respond, Bobby shouted, "I'm really, really, really happy!"

People laughed. Congregants began gathering their winter coats, and well wishes and shouts of "Merry Christmas" echoed in the foyer. I leaned my head on Micah's shoulder, and Bobby wrapped an arm around each of us. As Micah's arm encircled my waist, I whispered back, "Yes, I am truly happy. It's the greatest Christmas ever."

"Yeah," Bobby shouted, "the greatest Christmas ever!"

Also by GAYLE M. IRWIN

Montana Pet Rescue
Highwood Holiday

Pet Rescue Romance
Rescue Road
My Montana Love
In the Shadow of Mount Moran
Paws-itively Love
Pet Rescue Romance - Yellowstone Country Boxed Set
Finding Love at Compassion Ranch
Grams' Legacy
Rhiann's Rescue - Pet Rescue Romance Series Prequel
Paws-ing for Love: A Pet Rescue Christmas Story

Wyoming Pet Rescue Romance
Tails of the Heart

Standalone

Love Takes Flight

Watch for more at https://gaylemirwin.com/.

About the Author

Gayle M. Irwin is an award-winning author and freelance writer. She is a contributor to seven *Chicken Soup for the Soul* books and the author of inspirational pet books for children and adults, including the Pet Rescue Romance series, a collection of sweet, contemporary romance stories set in the Rocky Mountain West. She weaves life lessons within the pages of her works, including courage, kindness, perseverance, friendship nature appreciation, and the importance of pet rescue and adoption. She volunteers for rescue organizations and donates a percentage of book sales to such groups. Her own pets are rescues that she and her husband adopted. Learn more about Gayle and her writing at www.gaylemirwincom..

Read more at https://gaylemirwin.com/.

9 798227 691996